THE EXECUTIONER . . .

The man was in his late twenties, slim and blond and erect. His suit sat well on him, expensive cloth hanging from good shoulders.

He walked in a springy way. His expression was that of a man just about to smile. He looked alert and intelligent, like any successful young businessman.

His had been a spectacular career, dating from his first and only prison term at the age of twenty-one. In seven years he had killed twelve men and two women.

He arrived in the sleepy town of Flamingo, Florida, on April thirteenth.

He had a job to do . . .

JOHN D. MacDONALD

APRIL EVIL

FAWCETT GOLD MEDAL • NEW YORK

APRIL EVIL

Published by Fawcett Gold Medal Books, a unit of CBS Publications,
the Consumer Publishing Division of CBS Inc.

ISBN: 0-449-14128-4

Printed in the United States of America

17 16 15 14 13 12 11 10 9

The couple arrived in Flamingo, a town of twelve thousand population on Florida's west coast, at about eleven-thirty on the morning of the eleventh of April. They arrived in a gray Buick sedan with Illinois plates. The big car was dirty after the long trip. Racked clothing hung in the back.

The gray Buick cruised the main shopping section on Bay Avenue for a few minutes and then pulled into a drive-in restaurant on the west end of Bay Avenue near the approach to the causeway and bridge that led to Flamingo Key.

It was a hot day, too hot to eat in the car. There was no one in the other cars. The other customers were all inside the restaurant. A waitress in a green cotton uniform stood in the angular patch of shade made by the building itself, her back against the pink wall, and watched the couple as they got out of the gray car. She smoked a cigarette and watched them and wondered idly about them.

The man was tall. He was about thirty years old. He had the look of someone still recovering from a serious illness. He slid carefully out from behind the wheel and stood by the car, his posture bad, shoulders thrust forward. He wore a white shirt with the sleeves rolled up and the collar open, gray pants that were baggy at the knees. The shirt and trousers looked as though they had been made for a larger man. The trousers were gathered at the belt line and hung slack in the back.

He stood blinking in the bright sunshine, his shadow black against the blue-black of the asphalt. His color was not good and the glossy black of his hair seemed the most alive thing about him. He stood and looked toward the causeway. He rubbed his left arm and elbow gingerly. It was pink from the sun, from resting on the sill of the car window as he drove.

The woman was still in the car, putting on lipstick. The man turned and looked up Bay Avenue toward the shopping section, and then turned farther and looked at the waitress. There were deep lines in his cheeks. There were dark patches under hot dark eyes. His nose was long, thin at the bridge, wide at the nostrils. He looked at the waitress with a complete lack of expression. That is not something often seen. The dead wear no expression. Neither do the victims of dementia praecox when in catatonic state. Something behind the face looked out of the dark eyes at her, and the face told her nothing. The waitress felt oddly uncomfortable. She was a handsome husky girl, accustomed to stares, but not of that sort. She looked away.

The man spoke in a low impatient voice to the woman in the car. She got out quickly. She was a tall girl of about twenty-five, as tall as the man in her high heels. She wore a sheer white blouse. Her tan linen skirt was badly wrinkled. She smoothed it across her hips with the back of her hand. Her blonde hair was cropped short, and the waitress decided it was not becoming to her. It made the girl's face look too large, too heavy. The girl had the wide cheekbones, the short upper lip, the wide-set blue eyes, the heaviness of mouth that have become a stereotype of sensual beauty. Her tall figure was good, but slightly heavy. There was a look of softness about it. Her legs were very white. The girl's face was passive, with a hint of almost bovine endurance. She walked in an oddly constricted way. It was a walk in which there was body-consciousness and a flavor of humility. She walked as though she half expected a sudden blow, and yet would not mind too much if it came.

The man locked the car quickly and passed the girl on the way to the door and held it open for her. The waitress snapped her cigarette out onto the asphalt. She thought that the couple had not had a very good trip. It looked as though the girl had gotten the wrong man, and that was too bad. But a lot of us get the wrong ones. And it's too late then and not much you can do about it. There are more wrong ones than right ones.

The waitress went in the side door of the restaurant. The man had taken a paper from the rack by the door. They had taken a table for two. The man read the morning Flamingo *Record*. The waitress was glad it was not her table. The girl sat quite still and looked beyond the man, out the big side window toward the blue water of the bay and the white houses on the key beyond the bay. At intervals she lifted a cigarette slowly to her mouth, and as slowly returned it to hold it over the chipped glass ashtray on the formica table.

By two o'clock, using the name Mr. and Mrs. John Wheeler, the couple had rented the Mather house on the bay shore three miles south of the center of town. Hedges, the realtor, had tried to interest them in a house on the key, but they had not wanted to be on the key. The Mather house was long, low—a three-bedroom two-bath cypress house with a terrace that faced the bay, a new dock but no boat. The nearest house north of it was over two hundred feet away, and almost entirely screened by dense plantings. The vacant land south of the house was thickly overgrown with palmetto and cabbage palm and weeds.

The Mather house had a curving shell drive, live oaks heavy with Spanish moss, some delicate punk trees, a few pepper trees, a clump of coconut palm. There was a phone in the house on temporary disconnect, and Hedges promised to have it hooked up that same day. The man had paid in cash, seven hundred and seventy-two dollars and fifty cents. This included the three per cent state tax. It covered the rental up to May fifteenth.

After the transaction was complete, Bud Hedges, not a very imaginative or sensitive man, wondered why he should have strange fancies about the couple. They had not responded to any of his eager listing of the delights of a vacation in Flamingo. Even the dusty gray car had seemed blunt and sullen. He wondered why he had taken the precaution of jotting down the number from the Illinois plates. He shrugged off his strange feelings. The money was in hand. Mrs. Mather would be pleased. He had made thirty-seven-fifty for an hour of work during the month when the tourist season was ending. And the Wheelers had gotten what they wanted, a house with a maximum of privacy. He had not expected them to pay that much freight. The man's shoes had been black, cheap, cracked across the instep. Hedges always looked at their shoes. It was a better index than automobiles. You couldn't buy shoes on time.

They looked the house over more carefully after Hedges had gone. They carried the luggage in. The man wandered around the grounds while the girl unpacked. He went down and stood on the dock. Mullet jumped in the bay. A man in a yellow boat with a very quiet outboard motor trolled in a wide circle. A gray cabin cruiser went south by the channel markers. He could see the narrow pass between Flamingo Key and Sand Key, see the deeper blue of the waters of the Gulf of Mexico beyond the pass.

The girl came out on the front terrace and called to him. "It's all unpacked. We got to get some stuff."

He walked up to the terrace. "Like what?"

"You know. Staples. Bread and butter and eggs and cans and stuff."

"Can you cook?"

"I can cook some. You don't want to go out much, do you?"

"No. I don't want to go out much."

"I fixed the trays and turned the 'frig on high. There ought to be ice pretty quick."

"Little homemaker."

"Well . . . hell."

"Pick up a couple bottles too. Here."

She took the money. He heard the car leave a few minutes later. He paced through the empty house. He turned on a radio in the big kitchen. He found soap operas, hill-billies and Havana stations. He turned it off, drank a glass of water, frowned at the sulphur taste. He tried the phone but it wasn't hooked up yet. He went in and tested the beds. They felt all right. He took a shower. After the shower he dressed in the cotton slacks and aqua sports shirt he had picked up in that store in Georgia. He looked at himself in the full-length mirror as he combed his black glossy hair.

"Tourist," he whispered. And he grinned.

She drove in a few minutes later. He went out and carried half the stuff back in.

"Buy them out, baby?"

"It isn't as much as it looks like. It won't last long. Here's the bottles."

The ice was ready. He made himself a drink, and leaned against the sink and watched her putting the groceries away. She looked serious and intent and important.

"A new side to your character, baby," he said.

She straightened up and looked around. "It's a nice kitchen, Harry."

"It ought to be a nice kitchen. It ought to have a gold stove yet. It ought to have a floor show. Make with a floor show."

She gave him a sidelong look, and broke into a husky fragment of a chorus routine, ending with grind and bump. He put his glass down and clapped his hands solemnly three times.

"I'm out of practice," she said. She looked at him and then at her arms and said, "We ought to get some tan."

"You get some tan. This sunshine routine doesn't grab me."

"You'd look more like the other people around here."

"You wouldn't be trying to tell me my business."

"Don't get like that, Harry."

"Stick to cooking, Sal."

"Okay. Okay."

He left the kitchen and went to the phone again. He dialed zero. When the operator answered he hung up. He went to the bedroom and got the slip of paper from the top of the bureau and went back to the phone. He dialed the number.

"Sandwind Motel."

"Have you got a Robert Watson registered?"

"Yes sir, we have."

"I want to talk to him."

"I think he's on the beach right now."

"Can't you get him?"

"It might take some time. Why don't you give me your name and number and I can have him call you back."

"Okay. Tell him to call 9-3931." He hung up. He went out to the kitchen and made a fresh drink. Sal wouldn't look at him.

"For Christ sake don't sulk."

"Well, it's just that . . ."

"When Ace gets here keep your mouth shut. Don't talk. Get out of the way and leave us alone."

"Sure, Harry."

"You got the stuff put away?"

"Yes."

He slapped the seat of her wrinkled skirt. "Go get the happy sunshine, kid. Go brown yourself."

It was fifteen minutes before the phone rang.

The familiar voice said, "Hello?"

"Don't talk. That must be a hell of a big beach, Ace. I got a place. You check out of there and come on over here. Make it after dark. It's a house on a street called Huntington Drive. Eight hundred and three. There's posts by the driveway and a sign on the posts says Mather."

"You know I haven't got a car."

He paused a moment and said, "Okay. I see what you mean. Where is that damn place?"

"On Flamingo Key. You get on the main road on the key and turn left. You'll see it on the right."

"When does it get dark here?"

"A little after seven."

"Okay. I'll pick you up at seven-thirty. Gray Buick. That'll be better than some damn nosy cab driver."

"Did . . . did it go all right?"

"Silk and cream. No heat. We'll talk later."

Sally came out of the bedroom in the skimpy pale blue sunsuit she had bought in Georgia. She carried a blanket, a small brown bottle of sun lotion and a TV fan magazine.

"Okay?" she said.

"You're not what I'd call bundled up, kid."

He watched through the glass jalousies as she walked down to the dock, spread the blanket out, sat on it and began to carefully anoint her white legs and arms and shoulders and midriff. She stretched out in the glare of the afternoon sun, quiet as a corpse. The fish jumped. Wind ruffled the bay water. Harry made another drink. He felt restless. He tried to take a nap. He gave up and went down onto the dock. He took the aqua shirt off and sat near her in the sunshine. Maybe she was right about getting a tan. His skin was dead white. His ribs showed. There was a small mat of black hair on his chest. He sat hugging his knees. His shoulder blades stuck out in an angular way. There were two deep dimples on the back of his left shoulder, the scars of bullet wounds.

She lay on her back with her eyes shut. Her legs had turned pink. He looked at her legs and remembered something from one summer during an almost forgotten childhood. He reached out and pressed a finger against the top of her thigh. When he took it away the white spot faded slowly.

"You got enough. Get in the house."

"But Harry, I . . ."

His voice became very soft. "You're having a big day, kid. Homemaking and sulking and arguing. You want we should have a little trouble with you?"

She got up without another word and went up to the house. He stayed there another fifteen minutes. He folded the blanket and took it up to the house with him.

She had changed to a blouse and skirt. "I'm glad you told me when to quit," she said humbly. "I feel kind of prickly all over."

"I tell you everything you do."

"Sure, Harry."

"Then we don't have any trouble at all. There isn't going to be any room for any more trouble than the trouble I came for."

She lowered her voice. "Is it going to be rough?"

"Silk and cream, if it's done right. And it's going to be done right. I'm going to see that it's done right. The Ace and Ronnie are top talent. When it's done we split right away. Where they scatter is their problem. I know what direction we go in."

"Where do we go?"

"You know how I feel about questions."

"I'm sorry."

"I'm going to be able to use you. I figured it all out. When it's time I'll tell you what you have to do. It will be easy to do."

"Can I ask just one question? Just one?"

"All right. One."

"Harry . . . is anybody going to get killed?"

He buttoned his aqua shirt slowly. "I hope not, honey. I hope nobody gets killed. I hope nobody gets that excited."

CHAPTER TWO

Ben Piersall was late getting to the Flamingo Country Club and knew he would only have time for nine holes before dusk. He had phoned the club when he knew he would be late, and left word for the other members of the regular Monday foursome to tee off without him. He changed in the locker room, unfolded the caddy cart and walked out to the first tee, his cleats noisy on the duck boards, then silent on the grass.

He was a tall man, big in the shoulders, with a blunt, tanned, good-humored face, quiet gray eyes, brown hair that had begun to get a little bit thin on top. He had a successful law practice in Flamingo and he worked hard at it. He was a son of one of the town founders, and estate work made up a large percentage of his practice.

He saw that once again he would have to play alone. It seemed to be happening too often lately. He was losing the edge of his game. He snapped on his glove, teed up the ball, and took a few practice swings to loosen up. The club course was a flat course. The fairways were sun-baked. They would become increasingly hard and brown until the rains came in July. The first hole was three hundred and thirty-five yards, a par four with a well-trapped green and a narrow fairway.

His drive started low and began to climb. As it began to fall it developed a little tail and took a long long roll on the hard fairway. It rolled a bit beyond the three hundred marker. He had been the best man on the golf team when he had been in college. After school he had played in a few amateur tournaments, and had done well enough to toy with the idea of going on the regular tournament circuit. When he was able to play regularly he could still give Barney, the club pro, a good match. In his hottest round he had come within one stroke of the course record.

He knew his own weakness, and was amused by it. A lot of the frustrations of the day could be cleared away by really lacing into one, really pounding one. He could lower his score by holding back on the last few ounces of effort. But it was more satisfying to play it wide open. And there was a juvenile pride in knowing he could outdrive anyone in the club, including Barney, when he really got hold of one. Like that June day when, with a tail wind, and a fairway like concrete, he had overdriven the four hundred and ten yard twelfth hole. Fritz, in mock awe, had proclaimed that he intended to have a bronze marker placed where that incredible drive had come to rest.

Ben knew his big husky body needed regular exercise. He knew that he needed the complete relaxation that came after the shower and the drive home. It was more pleasure to play with the others, but better to play alone than not to play at all.

He dropped the iron shot five feet from the pin and canned the putt for his birdie. Playing alone there was no need to mark a card. He was a minus one thus far, and anticipated finishing the nine somewhere around par plus two or three.

When he walked onto the fourth tee, still one under, he saw a caddy cart about a hundred and seventy yards out, on the right side of the fairway. There was a bright red bag on the cart. He saw no player. He teed up and drove, getting a bit too much under the ball, wasting distance with too much altitude.

When he had walked about a hundred yards, the woman came out of the brush, club in hand. He recognized Lenora Parks. She took a new ball from the red bag and tossed it out and waited for him.

"You all alone, Ben?" she called as he came toward her.

"The assassins took off without me."

"Let's play along together then. That dang slice. I think I could have found it, but something rustled in there. I kept thinking of snakes. Maybe you can smell out that dang slice."

"Let's see."

She took a number three wood from her bag, waggled it, squinted at the green and swung. The ball, crisply hit, streaked up the center of the fairway and then faded right.

"See?"

"Sure. You've changed your stance, Lennie. It's too open. You're trying to steer the ball. Close the stance and just hit it. Don't think about a slice or think about trying to compensate for it by aiming left. It just makes it worse."

"Old Doctor Piersall's home remedy."

"It will work."

They walked up to his ball and she waited while he played a four iron all the way to the edge of the green.

"Wow!" she said. "You haven't lost your sock, old Ben. Remember how we used to play all the time?"

"Sure I remember."

They played along together. His advice worked. She was delighted. Lenora Parks was one of the better women golfers in the club. She was a dainty blonde woman with a figure still as good as it had been at eighteen, when they had gone together for over a year, back when she had been Lennie Keffler, before she married Dil Parks. It made him feel guilty and uncomfortable to play with her. Joan was quite aware of the past romance with Lennie. Joan had a cold eye for Lennie. And that was Lennie's fault, as Joan was not a particularly jealous wife. He and Joan kept running into Lennie and Dil at too many big parties. And Lennie, after the second drink, seemed to take a very proprietary attitude toward Ben Piersall. Ben suspected Lennie did that on purpose, knowing that it would cause Joan to give Ben a bad time. There was mockery in her eyes when she did it. He had long since guessed that it was a form of revenge. Theirs had been quite a turbulent affair, and he was the one who had ended it. He was careful not to stand alone with Lennie at any of the parties.

Dil Parks was about ninety-five per cent slob. Lennie had married him on the rebound from Ben. Lennie had made little bits of trouble here and there between her husband and herself. There was those in Flamingo who excused her on the grounds that a steady diet of Dil would drive anybody into the wrong bed. The other faction had a higher regard for marriage, Dil or no Dil. There had never been any actual proof of her inconstancy. The closest thing to proof was the garbled stories which came back from New Orleans the time three couples had gone over to Mardi Gras. But some of that could be blamed on inadequate reservations, three couples going when there were only reservations for two. Other comment was mostly locker room talk.

It made him feel uncomfortable to be with her, and he hoped that Joan wouldn't hear about it. He did not see how he could have gotten out of it gracefully. When he walked behind her and saw her trim hips under the pleated skirt, and saw her blonde hair bobbing as she walked, it seemed that she was exactly the same as the girl of eighteen summers—sixteen years ago. He remembered her mannerisms well enough to know that she was striking poses for him, displaying herself for him, trying in small delicate ways to arouse desire. But he knew that he would have none of that. Nor would he make any attempt even to find out if it was still available. He thought instead of the wrinkles at the corners of her eyes, the faint lines bracketing her mouth—and the grotesque and entirely unforgettable scene she had made at the time they had broken up.

But she was an attractive woman, and he knew that under the fragility, the blonde demureness, she was a most earthy woman. And he knew that he was making at least one concession to that by showing off. Like a boy chinning himself on a limb. He relished the little squeal she made when he hit a tremendous towering six iron shot that nearly holed out for an eagle.

"Remember the day we played sixty-three holes of golf, Ben?"

"The day before that dance?"

"I was so dang tired I thought I was going to go to sleep dancing with you."

"You slept all the way home."

. She tilted her head and grinned at him. "Not *all* the way home."

"Your putt."

"Poor old Ben. You get so stuffy and flustered. We're all grown up now, aren't we? Don't you think we are?"

"I guess so."

"That was all kid stuff."

"Watch yourself. This green is faster than the others."

She sat on her heels and lined the putt up. She stepped up to the ball, stroked it delicately. It ran twelve feet, hit the back of the cup and dropped.

"Nice putt!"

"I always used to play better when I played with you. I always used to do everything better."

"Drop the needle, Lennie."

"Needle? Gosh sakes, I wouldn't needle old Ben."

But there had been enough needle so that his drive on the ninth put him 'way over in the rough behind some cabbage palms. He could see the green through a two-foot gap between the palm trunks. He tried a two iron and nearly decapitated himself when the ball came back off a palm trunk like a bullet. It put him far enough back and gave him a better lie. So he gambled on getting enough of a slice with a number four wood. It sliced all right and left him in the deepest trap on the course. He didn't get enough sand and left himself with a thirty-foot putt. He holed out for the six, which put him one over par for the nine.

"Ben, I want to talk to you."

"What about?"

"Go take your shower first. I'll be on the porch. This will be a business conversation."

"Those belong in the office."

"Don't be so stuffy. Do you know you're getting terribly stuffy lately? You're afraid it will get back to Joan. You can tell her it was business, and tell her just what business it was, if lawyers' wives get in on lawyers' secrets."

Again he couldn't get out of it gracefully. When he came out onto the porch Lennie sat in one of the big chairs in the dusk. She had her drink in her hand and there was one for him on the round table between the two chairs. But for them, the porch was empty.

"Scotch old-fashioned? Is that right?"

"That's a habit that hasn't changed, Lennie. What's on your mind?"

"It's something I don't like, Ben. It's about Dil's uncle."

"Doctor Tomlin is Dil's great uncle, actually."

"Oh, I know that. But Dill is his closest living relative."

"They don't get along."

"That isn't our fault," she said hotly. "My God, I've tried. Your father used to handle Paul Tomlin's legal business. Do you handle it now?"

"I guess I would if he had any."

"Is there a will?"

"There may be. I don't know. I didn't handle it. Even if I did, I couldn't tell you what was in it."

"That isn't what was on my mind. I know better than that. It's something else."

She was leaning toward him. The fading light was odd against her face, slanting, showing bone structure. "Ben, you know how he is. He's nearly eighty. He's been quite mad for years."

"Eccentric."

"You use that word because he's rich. If he was poor you'd say mad and he would have been put away."

"He's not that bad."

"You don't know how bad he is. Have you heard about that couple?"

"They're relatives, aren't they?"

"They claim to be. Fiftieth cousins or something. Dil never heard of them. Dil and I have been over all that genealogy stuff his mother was so interested in before she died. We can't trace them accurately. There are people named Preston in the family. These people claim their name is Preston. We didn't know anything about it until he'd taken them in. I can't understand his taking anybody into that . . . that damn fortress with him. But he did. He's senile, Ben. God only knows what they're telling him, what they're getting out of him."

"I heard some relatives had moved in with him. I thought it was strange at the time."

"It *is* strange. And Dil is so dang wishy-washy. He doesn't want to *do* anything. I was going to come and see you in the office. Maybe this is better, to run into you here."

"What can you do? You can't run those people out. They're his guests."

"Face it. He's quite mad. We're his nearest relatives. I think it's high time we ought to start proceedings and get him committed."

She waited in silence for his answer. Ben thought it over a long time. The longer he thought, the less he liked it. "I wouldn't have any part of anything like that. He isn't a menace to anybody. Lennie, you're just damn scared that those Prestons are going to cut you out. It's just greed talking."

"Say no if you want to, but don't get moralistic."

"Maybe you can get somebody to try it. But you're going to get your nose bumped. He's an impressive old duck. He'd talk well at a hearing. It would fall through and you'd guarantee you would get nothing when he dies."

"When he dies. Sometimes it seems as if I've been waiting half my life for him to die."

"Dil had his chance with the old man. Dil just didn't take it."

"If anybody could do it, Ben, you could. He's really mad. You know that. We would . . . meet any fee you ask."

"I'm not that hungry."

"But that money! Isn't that enough? Isn't that enough evidence?"

"There's no law that says you have to keep money in a bank. There's no law that says you can't turn your home into a vault and guard it. He lost money twenty years ago when the bank closed. He decided he wouldn't lose it that way again. And remember, Lennie, there's a lot of people around here who were treated by him when he was still practicing. He has quite a backlog of good will. Suppose you did get him put away. There'd be talk. You'd find it tough to keep on living here."

"With that money we wouldn't have to live here."

"It couldn't be touched until his death, anyway."

In a voice so low he could barely hear her, she said, "The change would probably kill him."

"That's pretty vicious, Lennie."

"It's realistic. What good is it to him? We've been living over our heads for years. Counting on that money. Do you know what we owe? Never mind. It's a fine fat figure. The agency would have to sell a hundred cars tomorrow to get us out of deep water. Now summer's coming up. I frankly don't know how we're going to squeak through, honestly. Dil even tried to borrow from Uncle Paul. Hah! That was a big fat mistake. I'm looking out for myself, Ben. I'm so dang sick of everything. I am."

"But you haven't hit on the way out. That's a bad idea."

"Got a better one? Got any kind of an idea?"

"No."

"Somebody will help, Ben. Somebody will try it."

"Probably. Not me."

"Thanks for everything. You're so sweet."

"Thanks for the drink. I've got to run."

"Give Joan my very best love."

She went down the wooden porch, heels clacking. He saw her again after she went down the steps, walking toward the parking lot, her hair pale against the shadows of dusk.

He left the two empty glasses there on the table and walked slowly out to his car. He'd had no idea things were that bad with Dil and Lenora. But they wouldn't get away with pulling anything that raw. Not in Flamingo.

To an outsider it might seem that Dr. Paul Tomlin was beyond the elusive borderline of sanity. Those who knew him knew that he was merely proud, independent, stubborn. He had come to Flamingo to practice in 1900, when the town was young. After he had established himself, his wife and young son had died of undulant fever. The loss had soured him, set him apart from other people. His niece and her husband, Dil's parents, had come down to keep house for him. Dil's father, Wes Parks, had established himself in the real estate business. Dr. Tomlin had worked long dogged hours. He had believed in the eventual growth of Florida's west coast. Whenever he had a little money ahead, he put it into gulf front land, often accepting Wes Parks' advice and just as often ignoring it.

When the bank had closed he had not lost much money, but he had lost enough to disabuse him of banks. By working harder he managed to retain all the land he had purchased, and even buy more. When, in 1934, the causeway to Flamingo Key had been built, Dr. Tomlin owned over three thousand yards of gulf-to-bay frontage. He had bought some of it for as little as ten dollars an acre. That land in the hands of the present owners was worth nearly two hundred dollars a front foot.

Dr. Tomlin had not begun to sell off his land in any quantity until 1940, the year he retired. With the proceeds of the first ninety thousand dollar sale he had built Rocklands, the fortress house, on a knoll two miles inland from the center of Flamingo. It was built of native stone and surrounded by a high wall. A safe was brought down from Birmingham by technicians and built into the house during construction. He lived there alone with a Negro named Arnold Addams, who, as a young man, had driven the doctor's car during the last few years of his practice, and was now a husky graying man who ran errands and drove the doctor to town on his rare business dealings.

Most of the property had been sold. The last big pieces were sold in 1950 and 1951. In 1951 the Flamingo Bank and Trust Company had had to arrange through Tampa for the money necessary to cash the check Dr. Tomlin had presented.

The doctor was a recluse. Few people had been inside the great stone house. They told conflicting stories of what they saw. Arnold Addams was a completely loyal and close-mouthed man. The rumors of the amount of money in the big safe were fantastic. Ben Piersall was inclined to believe that Bud Hedges came closest to an accurate guess. Hedges had looked up all the old real estate transfers. He had deducted probable taxes, the cost of the big house, probable living expenses. Hedges estimated that the old man must have somewhere between one million three and one million five squirreled away in the big safe, all in cash. Hedges had investigated carefully to be certain Tomlin had not re-invested the money.

Tomlin was coldly polite to the people he came in contact with. The car Addams drove was a black pre-war Packard, polished to a high luster. It was the same car he had used in the last few years before his retirement from the practice of general medicine. From time to time cases of books and phonograph records would arrive at the railway express station, and Arnold Addams would drive down and pick them up.

No, Ben thought, there was nothing there on which to base the sort of proceeding Lennie contemplated. A man could drive an aged car if he wished. He could save his money in cash if he so desired. Tomlin was a tall, straight, frail old man, full of years and dignity. Wes Parks and his wife were many years dead. It had been generally conceded in town that Dil and Lennie Parks would inherit the cash. Too bad, but Dil would get his hands on it.

Now a new factor had been added. He could understand Lennie's distress, and her greed—but not approve of it.

Dil had turned into a big-bellied, hard-drinking loudmouth. It was not a role that suited him with precision. There was something plaintive and uneasy in his eyes, even as he told his bawdiest stories. He owned and operated a marginal automobile agency. He was difficult to work for. People did not stay with him long. Dil and Lennie were childless.

Ben Piersall drove home to Huntington Drive. He was much later than usual after golf, and suspected he should have phoned. Toby's bike was in the garage, and, as he drove in, he saw Sue, his just-turned-fourteen daughter through the living room picture window adjusting the dials of the television set. He went through the garage into the kitchen. Joan was standing frowning at the refrigerator.

She turned and smiled at him and they kissed. She was a tall pretty woman with Indian black hair, tan face, and eyes of a hot bright startling blue. She was broad-shouldered and high-waisted and long-legged and she moved in a pliant and, to Ben, continually provocative way.

"Playing in the dark? Luminous golf ball? Or a hard round on the nineteenth hole?"

"I missed the guys. Too late. Played nine alone." He took a deep breath. "Not quite alone. Caught up with Lennie on the fourth and got trapped into finishing out with her."

It was the best way, he decided, even though the blue eyes did frost over. "Trapped, as you so neatly put it. There is poisoned bait in that cute little trap."

"I'm immune, honey."

"I hope you are. I really do."

"She had some business to talk over. I'll tell you after the kids are in bed. A stinking deal. She wants to commit Paul Tomlin."

Joan's eyes narrowed. "Very, very typical. So she came running right to you. Good old Ben. Pal of her cradle days."

"I said no."

"Of course. Darling, this misbegotten failure of a refrigerator has stopped defrosting again. I feel like kicking it. Please call them in the morning and jump on them. They'll listen to you quicker. This is not one of the best days. Sue is being plaintive about going to the movies on a school night."

"No."

"I told her that too. And Toby had an experience."

Toby came into the kitchen then. "Hi, Dad. She's right. An experience. Brother!"

"He didn't know the Mather house next door had been

rented. Neither did I. I guess they took it today. When he got home from school he . . ."

"Gee, Mom, let me tell it. I took the spinning rod and went over on the dock. I just had time to hit the tide change. I figured on maybe a red in that hole out there. I just got to make one cast and this real mean guy comes running down out of the house. He says to me, just like this, 'Get the God damn hell off this property.' He looked like some kind of gangster, honest. He looked like he was going to hit me. I tried to say I didn't know it had been rented, and he just said it again. So . . . I came home. There's a woman there too. I saw her through the window. She was looking out. You know who she kind of looks like? That Dagmar on the television."

"We'll see about this," Ben said.

He went to the phone and got hold of Hedges at his home. "Bud? This is Ben Piersall. You've got an exclusive on that Mather house. I thought we had a gentleman's agreement about what you'd put in there. What kind of people have you got in there now?"

"Their name is Wheeler. I think they're okay. That's a tough property to rent when it gets to be . . ."

"I don't care how tough it is. The man cussed out Toby. Toby went over to the dock there. He didn't know it was rented. The man was profane and abusive."

"I'm sorry as hell about that. I thought it would be all right because they were so insistent on complete privacy. I don't think they'll bother you at all. They're Illinois people. Just down until May fifteenth. She's quite a dish, boy."

"Put the butter away, Bud. I'm a little annoyed."

"You've got a right to be. I should have phoned Joan and told her. I had it on my mind but I forgot it. It's my fault."

Ben Piersall was mollified. They chatted about other matters. He hung up, and went back to the kitchen. "Hedges was trying to make that fast buck. The Wilkinsons paid a season rate and left last week. The odds were against it renting again. We and the kids just stay away from these Wheelers. That clear, Toby?"

"Gosh, I wouldn't go over there again."

Sue was firmly informed that there would be no school-night movie. She phoned her girl friend to say it was off. She tried to maintain an attitude of chilly indifference, haughty resignation, a princess condemned to dine with the palace serfs, but she forgot her role after a half-hour.

Ben mixed a drink before dinner. After dinner he read while Joan and Sue did the dishes and Toby did homework. The kids went to bed at nine-thirty with the usual token protests. When he and Joan were alone in the living room, he put his book aside and told her the details of the conversation with Lenora Parks.

"Could they do such a thing?"

"It's unlikely—unless Doctor Tomlin has failed pretty badly in the last two months. I haven't seen him since sometime in January."

"How can she and Dil even think of doing a thing like that?"

"It's more Lennie than Dil. She's restless . . . and ruthless."

"She's a bad person, Benjamin."

He thought that was not entirely accurate, but he had no stomach for arguing on Lennie's side. It wasn't badness. More it was a misdirected strength. He was glad that he had not married Lenora, as he had seriously considered doing at one time. He liked kids, for one thing. When Dil was younger he had been in the sort of jam that decisively proved his fertility. It was evident that Lennie was the barren one. In spite of her hungers there seemed to be a curious sterility about her. It would have been a sterile life for Ben without Joan in any event. Inconceivable without Joan, without the special warmth of this marriage.

After Joan had gone to bed he walked slowly through the house, feeling smug about his home and the warmth it enclosed. These were the good years. He turned out the lights, evicted Buckethead, the calico cat, checked the locks. In the darkness he could see the gleam of lights in the Mather house, shining through the leaves. He felt a recurrence of the anger, wondered if he had let Toby down by not charging over there and demanding apologies. He shrugged and went to bed.

CHAPTER THREE

He parked just beyond the range of the floodlights of the Sandwind Motel. The Ace had been waiting and he came out quickly, walking with his heavy, plunging stride, his big shadow long in the white lights. He looked into the gray Buick and grunted in affirmation. He put the suitcase in the back, dropped into the front seat beside Harry and banged the door shut. He heaved his big body into a more comfortable position, the front seat creaking under his weight.

Harry made a wide U turn and headed back along the key toward the causeway road.

"Beach boy," Harry said. "Handstands for the girls."

"So it's like a vacation."

"When did you get down?"

"Nearly a week. Last Tuesday. How about this heap?"

"Don't sweat. It's clean. Riverio owed me a favor. Registration and license are okay. In the name of John Wheeler, with a Chicago address that'll check out, if nobody checks it too hard."

"And the kid?"

"Tomorrow or Wednesday. He comes in by train."

"How does he connect?"

"They've got a book at the Chamber of Commerce. A notebook like. For messages. In the morning you go down and put the address in. . . . No, you put the phone number in. Ronnie will look for it there."

"You got a date set up?"

"Not yet. We got to ease into this. No slips. This might be as big as Boston."

"You kidding?"

"No. I'm not kidding. And one thing straight, Ace. I'm running it. All the way."

"That was the way I heard it."

"I've got a woman with me."

Ace was quiet for a few moments. "I don't like that a God damn bit."

"I don't care whether you like it or don't like it. I needed the cover on the way down. She's all right. She used to run around with Barney Shuseck."

"Barney's dead."

"Before they caught up with him, they had her on ice for a week. She gave them nothing."

"So he's still dead."

"That had nothing to do with her."

"I don't like it."

"You'll get used to it."

"With a woman around the kid is hard to handle."

"I'll handle Ronnie."

"How did you tie up with her?"

"I hid out at Riverio's place, at the lake. I was about to go nuts. He sent her up."

"If this cracks right, where you going?"

"I got to go out of the country. You know that much."

"I know. Did you get an address?"

"A couple of them."

"This what's-her-name. She going?"

"I don't know yet."

"Does she think she's going?"

"Yes."

"What's the scoop on this thing, anyway? The little I got, it sounded crazy. I almost didn't come. I'll say whether I'm in after you tell me the whole deal."

"You'll be in."

"I don't like working with the kid."

"We need the kid."

Ace stretched his big arms and yawned. "How did it feel to make the list?"

"Don't ride me, damn it!"

"Harry Mullin, one of the ten most wanted criminals."

"Ace, I'm telling you!"

"You are jumpy, boy. Ease off. Actually, how does it feel?"

"It feels like hell. They put those pictures too many places. Too many people got this hobby, checking those pictures. I took off twenty-five pounds. It helps some, but not enough. On the way down I felt like I ought to have my head in a bag. That's how it feels. Every time anybody looks at you, you wonder if they've been checking those damn pictures. So I stay the hell in the house."

"That nearly cooled me off too. It makes you too heavy. Then I thought what the hell. It'll just make you more careful."

"I'm careful."

"You weren't careful, Harry, when you killed that woman."

"I was careful. I was just unlucky. I fired at the floor. The damn bank had a marble floor. It bounced up and clocked her right under the chin. A fat lady."

"Real fat?"

"She was a hell of a big woman. I heard later she didn't even have any bank business. She just went in to use the john. And she wasn't the one yelling, the one I fired to shut up."

"Is this the place? Say, this is pretty fancy."

"It has to be. You stay in a crummy place, some cop looks you over. You stay in a place like this, they don't bother you."

He ran the Buick into the garage. They got out and Harry pulled the overhead door down. They went into the house through the garage, into the kitchen.

Sally Leon stood at the stove, stirring something in an aluminum pot. She smiled faintly at the two men as they came into the kitchen.

"Sally, this is the Ace." They nodded at each other. "Big bastard, isn't he?"

The Ace seemed to fill the kitchen. He was well over six feet tall and he was broad all the way down, with hardly any suggestion of a waist. He was in his early forties. The top of his head was shiny-bald, sun-reddened, surrounded by kinky ginger hair. His brows and nose and lips were thickened by early years in the ring. His jacket was expensive and well cut. His eyes were small and blue and bright. He looked as though he could have been an ex-pro-football linesman turned salesman.

"Whatever you got there, it smells good," Ace said.

"It's a beef stew like."

Harry Mullin made two drinks, gave one to Ace and they carried them into the living room.

"Nice deal. Pretty here. With the lights on those bushes. Where do I bunk?"

"There's two down that hall. Take either one."

"I'll get the bag later. If I decide to come in on this."

"You want the story now. Okay. The month before I crashed out, I got to know one of the new fish who'd just come in. He figured with me being in there four years already and being a lifer, I'd know all the scores. He was in on armed robbery, a supermarket in Evanston. He'd come in from the West Coast and it was the first thing he tried and he'd hooked up with the wrong guy so it went sour. He was all set on what he'd do when he got out, and he knew I couldn't ever be paroled so he thought it was safe to talk it over with me.

"It seems when he was out on the coast he had this good friend named Joe Preston. Preston was always getting into small time trouble. But Preston talks about some rich doctor in this town here, here in Flamingo, that he's related to. Preston and his wife leave. This fish, his name is Irv Dingle, gets a letter from Preston. Preston brags about the rich doctor relative. He says he and his wife have moved in with the old boy. He says the doctor doesn't believe in banks and he's made a killing in land and has maybe a million bucks in cash in the safe in his house."

"Sure. A million bucks. Ten or fifteen thousand."

"Wait a minute. Four years didn't soften me up. After Riverio hid me out I started thinking about it, wondering if it could be true. So I had Riverio run a check. He had somebody come over from Miami and look around. It gets checked a half dozen ways and it adds up to a minimum of a half million. Cash. It could be a hell of a lot more. He lives in a big stone house. The Preston couple and some old jig live there with the doctor. I couldn't get the dope on the kind of box, but it was put in twenty years ago."

"Then a torch and a can opener ought to do it."

"That's your business. But like I said, Riverio checked."

"I'll believe that. But why doesn't he assign it?"

"Because he hasn't got the people any more. There aren't many people around to handle it. He's been going legit. He's had his orders to go legit. The top-side wouldn't have liked it for him to hide me out, or even make this check, but as I said, he owed me a couple of favors. Now we're clear. I got to the cash I had stashed, and I've got enough to swing this thing. That was what Dingle was after in Evanston, the cash to finance this thing. Now I want to know if you're in."

The Ace picked up his glass and walked to the jalousied windows and looked toward the dark bay. Finally he shrugged big shoulders. "Sure."

"That's good. You're a good man with a box. There aren't many good ones left."

"But no killing."

"No killing."

"I've never been in on a score where there was any. And I don't want to start. That's why I don't like working with the kid."

"I can hold him down."

"How do you want to do it?"

"The easy way. Get in and take over the house. Maybe if we rough the old man up a little, we can open the box with the dial. We'll study the map and lay out a route. I figure Tampa would be a good place to split up."

"How do you cut it?"

"Expenses out and the balance three ways."

"Are you sure the cash is there?"

"I know this much. When he was selling off land a few years back, the bank used to send a guard right along with him, right to his door, when he was taking the cash home. What does that sound like?"

The Ace grinned. "It sounds sweet."

"This will go like cream and silk. All I worry about is why it hasn't already been knocked off. Maybe the talent doesn't get around this way."

Sally came to the door and said they could eat any time. The men went out to the booth in the kitchen alcove. She served them big portions of the steaming beef stew. The three of them ate in silence. After Ace had pushed his plate away and sugared his coffee, he said, "How did you make it out? I heard a lot of stories."

Harry looked at Sally. She kept her eyes down. He shrugged and said, "No harm in telling you. You know, they gave me those consecutive sentences. The way I worked it out, if I could live to be a hundred and sixty-five, I might get out. So the day I went in, I started planning. I kept my head down. If you make no trouble, you get to move around more.

"I decided right away I wanted no part of any big crash. That hostage business is no good. It never works out. I had to get out of there all by myself, all alone. And I did. But it took four years. I figured up once I spent twelve thousand hours thinking and planning. You think that hard, something has to give. And I couldn't try a long-shot chance, because that would foul me up if I was caught. It had to be as sure as I could make it."

"That's a maximum-security prison."

"You're telling me no news, Ace. I finally decided the best deal was with the state road trucks. They save money for the state by using the prison shop and prison labor. There's a tough smart inspection squad that checks each truck in and out. Once in a while they get some old crock of a truck that needs a lot of welding on the frame. I spent a whole year making the right contacts in the repair shop. I couldn't get in there myself. No lifers in the auto shop. It took a lot of organizing and a lot of pressure. It went wrong a couple of times. But not wrong enough to make anybody suspicious. The timing just went bad. It finally worked right. I got into the shop and hid behind a locker until I got the signal. Then I got under a truck and pulled myself up underneath. My contacts had welded a couple of handles up under there, and a bar I could rest my weight on. They'd built skirts on the side so I was up out of sight. I took the chance. The squad looked under the truck but they missed me when the state driver took the truck out. That damn driver was a cowboy. That bar nearly broke my back.

"I'd got out from under the truck and made a phone call, still wearing the dungarees I put on in the auto shop, and been picked up and was forty miles out of town before they even knew I was gone. They still don't know how I got out. Big mystery. Big headlines. They won't know until somebody spots those handles and that bar, and maybe they never will."

"Very sleek," Ace said.

"But it can't ever happen again. I couldn't ever get out again. They'd watch me too close. And here's news for you. I'm never going back in again. They're never going to shut any gates on me again. I'm out for good. This deal is going to work. I'm going to make it work. And I'm going to live fat until I'm ninety, live in a place where I can keep my thumb on my nose. I've lost too many times. And I've lost too many years."

Ace leaned back. "When you talk like that I don't like this so much."

"What do you mean?"

"You used to kid around. You used to make it the easy way. Now you're all strung up. You've got the shakes."

"Maybe I've changed."

"I don't like the shakes."

"When we place the bet, I won't be shaking."

Ace stood up. "Don't be."

"Sit down!" Ace shrugged and sat down. "I'm running this. Anything that sounds like an order, I give it. Maybe you better get out right now."

"Don't get your ass in an uproar."

"In or out. Come on. If you're in, you take orders."

"The older you get, the meaner you get. All right. I take orders. Now I get my bag. Then I unpack. Then I make a drink. Okay, chief?"

Harry relaxed visibly. "Okay, Ace."

The two men sat up after the woman had gone to bed. They talked of old names and old places. They were like two mercenaries speaking of lost battles in a war in which they didn't believe. The list of the fallen was long.

After Ace had gone to bed, Harry Mullin sat alone, a Havana station whispering over the radio. He finished a last drink and went to bed. The woman lay asleep in the restless moonlight, dark leaf shadows moving against the contours of her soft sleeping body. Mullin thought of the money. He thought of it with heat and ferocity. He thought of the money with a special intensity. With his thoughts at that peak, he awakened the drowsy and acquiescent girl.

CHAPTER FOUR

Dr. Paul Tomlin stood at the window in his dressing room which adjoined his second floor bedroom. He wore an ancient and comfortable dressing gown. It was ten o'clock on Tuesday morning, the twelfth day of April—a warm windy day. He stood looking down at the girl who, with trowel in hand, grubbed patiently at the flower bed in the corner of the wall.

Dr. Tomlin was a tall, straight, lean, knotted old man with large, veined, blotched hands, wattled throat, hard shelf of brow, thin white hair with a faint yellowish tinge to it. He felt a warmth within him as he watched the girl. She was on her knees, faded blue jeans taut across round young buttocks, her hair dark gold in the sun as she worked away. The flowers were growing for her, as they had never done for Arnold. Since she had come here the food had become more varied, more pleasant. Furniture appeared in more pleasing arrangements. The entire house seemed lighter and more alive.

He remembered the day the couple had arrived, a cold day of rain two days after Christmas. The fat-pine fire Arnold had built crackled in the study fireplace. Arnold had come in, dark face both thoughtful and dubious to say, "They's a couple of young folks here says they's kin to you, Doctor. Name of Preston."

He remembered a letter that had come nearly two months before, a letter written in pencil, mailed in California, and signed Joseph Preston. It had traced the remote relationship. Joseph Preston was the grandson of the doctor's wife's half-brother. The letter had said that Joseph and his wife might drive east some time to visit. The doctor had not answered the letter. Now they had come. He knew he could not turn them away without seeing them.

But he could certainly turn them away after token greetings.

Annoyed, he told Arnold to show them in. He stood up, his back to the fire, and waited for them. Arnold ushered the young couple in. They looked ill at ease. The young man came forward with forced joviality, hand extended. "I'm Joe Preston, Doc. I guess we're related."

Tomlin took the hand and released it quickly. "Distantly, I believe." He did not like the look of Preston. He had a weak, narrow face. His sideburns were long and the dark hair was long above his ears, combed heavily back. He wore a ranch shirt and jeans with the belt buckled on the side.

"You've got a nice place here, Doc. This is Laurie, my wife."

"Forgive me, but I detest being called Doc, if you don't mind." He nodded at the girl, half smiling. She stood just inside the doorway, her body tense, unsmiling. She was of medium height, sturdy in her cotton skirt and light sweater. Her hair was brown and sun streaked, her face broad but pretty, lightly freckled.

"Come on, Joe!" she said with quiet firmness. "Come on!"

"Wait up, honey. We only just got here."

"I want to leave right now. He doesn't want us here. He didn't answer the letter. You can see by the way he acts. Don't be so . . ."

"Hold it!" Joe Preston snapped.

Dr. Tomlin found himself liking the girl on sight. There was something about the way she stood, something about the strength in her face and her eyes that reminded him of his long-dead wife when she had been a young girl.

He smiled and heard himself saying, "Yes, please do 'hold it.' Won't you both sit down, please?"

"See?" Joe said to Laurie and sat down before she did, sighing expansively, legs spread, elbows hooked on the chair arms.

The girl sat on the edge of a straight chair.

"Are you on your way through?" Tomlin asked.

"I thought I'd look around right here," Joe said. He made an expansive gesture. "The West Coast is shot. Too full of people. All crawling over each other trying to find jobs. This looks like a better deal, Doc . . . Doctor. For a while we didn't think the old heap was going to make it, but it got us all the way across the U. S. and A., didn't it, baby?"

The girl nodded. She looked at the doctor and blushed and looked away. The doctor thought, with some surprise, *she is sensitive. This is embarrassing her. She knows what he is and what he's doing and she doesn't like it.*

In that moment he became curious about Laurie. It was as though some buried and forgotten part of him awakened. It was a painful rebirth. The death of his wife and child had been a blow from which he had never entirely recovered. He had wanted solitude, and found it. For years he had lost himself in work. Since retirement he had lived apart here in the stone house, with books and music and memories of a past so distant that now the memories were fragile, soft-hued, like the dry brown flowers pressed in old books. He waited patiently for death in the old house. He was both resentful of and intrigued by his stir of interest in the girl.

He heard himself say, "You two could stay here for a little bit while you look around. A few days." He heard Arnold's astonished grunt in the dimness of the hallway beyond the study.

"That's damn white of you, Doc . . . tor."

"We appreciate it very much," the girl said in a low voice.

That was the way it had started. And the two of them had lived in the house ever since. And he was not sorry. Not for one minute had he been sorry. In the beginning Arnold had grumbled as much as he dared about the extra work. But as Laurie took over more and more of Arnold's unwelcome duties, that complaint faded away.

Joe Preston was no good. On his regular trips to town to "hunt up a job," he managed to return dulled by beer, steps heavy on the stairs. He had no conversation, and only the most rudimentary manners. Some stirrings of primitive conscience made him try to "help out," but his efforts were fragmentary and soon forgotten. He seemed to have the attention span of a small child, but all the sexual energies of a healthy young ram. And he was in ram heaven. A solid roof, a lot of food, a firm-bodied young wife and the privilege of sleeping until noon.

For some time Paul Tomlin wasn't able to draw the girl out. When at last she began to talk he found that his plaintive hope had been correct. She had sharp native intelligence. She'd had very little schooling. Her manners and her sensitivity were innate. And this was a house of books and of music. This was a house of a thousand new doors, all open to her. It both pleased and amused the doctor to see the avidity with which she entered the new worlds, to sense her hungriness for new intellectual experience. He subtly guided her reading, the music, their conversations. At dinner Joe Preston would gulp his coffee and leave the table, glad to be away from conversation that bored him.

Laurie had taste and imagination. It was fun to talk to her. It underlined a loneliness within himself that he had never suspected.

He remembered the things she said. "I don't dig this Bartok. I mean I think I see what he's trying to do, but I don't think I like it."

"What do you think he's trying to do?"

"Make music into arithmetic. Sometimes the notes sound like . . . like a roof where a bunch of icicles hang off. They're all different lengths, and different sizes, but they're all icicles. There isn't anything to melt them. I don't mean music has to be schmaltzy. But . . . there has to be more than tricks."

Or—"Maybe I can see what this Hemingway is doing, Doctor Paul. He could take the very same scene and by describing it a different way each time he could make you feel different each time, make you feel like the people in the scene feel. That keeps him from having to try to tell you what the people are thinking."

Or—"The thing I like best in the books and in the poetry and in the music is when all of a sudden something comes up that makes you feel all prickly, the back of your neck and the backs of your hands, and you can't breathe deeply. It's like you recognize something you knew all along. Is that what they try to do to you?"

"That's what they want to do, yes. But few people ever respond that way. Too few people, Laurie."

They talked together a great deal. Paul Tomlin was able to ignore the depressing presence of Joe Preston for the sake of the delight he took in watching this girl grow and unfold and flourish. She made the more immediate relatives, Dillon and Lenora Parks, poor things indeed. As she grew in stature, the efforts of his guidance became more visible. He began to feel possessive, and also felt growth and change within himself.

He became more resentful of Joe's claims on her time and her body and her emotions. The quiet evenings would end when Joe would, with surly insistence, take her off to bed. It seemed shameful to him that this perceptive girl, this sensitive organism, should be chained to crassness, vulgarity and appetite.

One March day as they sat together on the garden bench, Paul Tomlin asked her about her husband.

"How did you meet him, Laurie?"

She looked at him and looked quickly away, and he suspected that she sensed the disapproval behind his words. She shrugged. "I was in a little town named Crystal, California. I was with my aunt. She's dead now. She was run over last year. I was seventeen, and I had to quit school. I worked in the lunch room in the bus station. Joe came to town with a crew. They were mapping some kind of irrigation project. I went out with him a few times. He got into trouble and they fired him. He was stranded there. He seemed so helpless. He wanted to get married. So . . . we got married."

"He doesn't seem right for you, Laurie."

"How can you say that? What makes a person right for another person? I love him. He needs me. He isn't very much, but he'd be even less without me. I make him feel he belongs somewhere. He knows there's someone on his side. He needs that. We had to leave Los Angeles. I guess you didn't know that."

"No, I didn't."

"He started getting money. He lied about how he got it. He was running around with the wrong people. A man named Dingle was a bad influence on him. Joe likes to act like a big shot. He was picked up. I found out he was working for a bookmaker. Then he was picked up again on suspicion of robbery. One of the police sergeants was nice to me. He said I ought to get Joe to leave. He said if Joe stayed in town he wouldn't stay free very long. He said we should leave. It might help Joe and it would save the state of California some money. That's why we left and why we came here."

"The small amounts of money I've given you for your personal use, Laurie. You've given some of it to him."

"He has to have *some* money in his pocket, even if it's only a dollar or two. I didn't want to take any money, anyway. I can get a job here. I've told you that, Doctor Paul."

"I don't want you to. You do enough right here, in this house."

"I don't do much of anything."

"Arnold thinks differently."

She smiled. "You two were in a rut. The same menu every week. The same routine. I'm afraid we've spoiled the routine."

"For the better."

"I should get a job. I feel like I'm sponging."

"You're not. Laurie, would you feel better if I gave you some sort of a title and regular pay? Housekeeper or something?"

"I . . . I might. But I didn't plan that we'd stay on here."

"I want you to. I think I need you here, Laurie. I needed to be stirred up."

At other times he told her about his life, about what

had happened to him. And one day when Joe had gone to town and Arnold was on an errand, he took her to the study, slid the paneling aside and showed her the big safe and its contents, the brown-wrapped bills stacked with the dusty profusion of magazines in a basement, behind and around the large tin box that held important papers.

He watched her face, saw her eyes go wide and then saw the puzzled frown.

"But why?" she asked. "It doesn't even look real. It seems . . . grotesque."

He closed the door of the safe, spun the dial. "I guess it is grotesque."

"Why do you keep all that here?"

"My dear, you can call it affectation. And a gesture of defiance. I treated their bodies for years, the people in this town. I knew their bodies well. The laboring lungs and the overworked hearts. The cancers and the infections. There is something impressive and awe-inspiring about the resiliency of the human body. I couldn't treat their bodies without learning about their minds, the way they thought. Bitterness and envy and greed. Dirty little machinations to gain this advantage and that. And their sorry little god was and is money.

"I was fortunate enough to make a great deal of money in land. I had captured their god. To their way of thinking, once the god has been chained, you put him to work for you. And he faithfully brings in your three per cent or your eight per cent, depending on the risk of the work you assign him to. It is inconceivable to them that once you have captured the god, you don't put him to work. So, as a gesture of defiance—probably childish—I imprisoned the god in this safe and would not let him work. There is enough there for a dozen lifetimes. There is no necessity to make him work for me. Whatever I spend, it comes out of capital. I suspect I am the only millionaire in the world with absolutely no income whatever.

"Perhaps it is a product of my original hurt—to defy the rules of the clan, break the taboos of the village. Through the years I have taken a certain satisfaction in being a man of mystery, in knowing that they whisper and point and envy me. It has been a source of wry pleasure to have them envy me for the possession of something I value very little. I am a contrived eccentric. It is my small revolt against society. Do you understand?"

"I think I do, Doctor Paul."

He closed the panel and said, "Locked away in here are the services the imprisoned god will perform for you. Cars and planes and cruises. Or charities that bear your name. All manner of gleaming things. But I won't play the game their way. Because of that they respect me and they despise me, and maybe it makes them doubt a little. This is a god who does not work."

"What will happen to it?"

"When I die? Don't blush, Laurie. It's a perfectly normal question. I will set up two trust funds. One will be for you. Then the balance will be divided among medical research organizations, with one lump sum set aside for taxes."

"I don't want it."

"Be honest, Laurie."

She smiled then. "Of course I want it. I don't want you to think that's why I asked."

"I don't."

"Then . . . thank you."

"With an income for the rest of your life, you can do as you please about Joe. You can support him or not, as you please. I suggest you'll be happier if you do not support him."

"There's something good about him. You don't see it."

"I'm afraid I don't."

He stood at the window and looked down at her as she worked in the yard. There was a new zest in living since she had come into his life. Had his child lived, this was the granddaughter he would have wanted. He went down the wide stairs and out the side door. She looked up as he approached.

"I never sleep late in the morning," she said, imitating his voice. "Good morning."

"We talked too late. Past my bedtime."

She stood up. "And now you need your breakfast. I sent Arnold off with a mile-long shopping list. You walk around in the sun. It will make you hungry. I'll whistle when it's ready."

She went into the house. The grounds enclosed by the high stone wall were not large. The sun was warm on the back of his neck. The garage doors were open, and the black Packard was gone. He could see Joe Preston's ancient car in the other stall, behind closed doors. Arnold lived over the garage. The curtains at his windows were crisply white. Tomlin walked down the drive and saw that the front gates were open. Before Laurie and Joe had come, Arnold Addams had been ceremonious about locking the gate each time he left the house. He seemed to feel there was security in added numbers.

Dr. Paul Tomlin stood in the entrance, his hands in the pockets of the robe. Across the narrow street there was an empty house, a relic of the boom of the twenties, a great crumbling yellow cement monstrosity, heavy with Mediterranean arches, bastard offspring of mixed Spanish and Moorish ancestry. Off to the left, beyond the sad yellow house, he could see the bright new homes of a low-cost housing development, houses in shades of raspberry and lime, aqua and peach. Homes with terrazzo, Floridy rooms, and coaxial television from a community aerial, with small yards afflicted by chinch bugs and sand spurs. Carport homes where once there had been dry flats with palmetto scrub and the raw grasses. Now the flats were bisected by the thin skin of asphalt, and robins in migration no longer rested there.

A car moved slowly down the narrow street. It was a travel-dusty Buick, with a big man behind the wheel who stared curiously at the doctor and at the stone house behind him. The doctor stared calmly back. The car speeded up after it had passed the house. He noted that it had Illinois plates.

CHAPTER FIVE

Through the glass of the office wall Mooney could see Dil Parks. Dil had a friend in there with him. Even though somebody was beating out a fender in the adjoining service garage, Mooney could hear the juicy ripeness of Dil Parks' laughter. Mooney moved to a place on the showroom floor where he could not see Parks and where he could hear him less. He reflected that he would dearly love to bust Parks firmly in the nose.

Mooney was a restless man, an itinerant auto salesman. He had broken in on the used car lots of Dayton and Cleveland and Columbus. He was forty and looked thirty. He was restless, unattached, world-wise. He knew he was no good on the long-term contract sales. He had no stomach for clubs, or golf games, or cocktail-party chatter. He knew he was the best floor man and best lot man he had ever seen. He could club the drifters. He felt alive when he was jamming the sale down their throats, making it taste sweet to them. He'd sharpened his weapons in Los Angeles, in Detroit, in the Bronx. He'd drifted down to Florida right after Christmas. And he'd unloaded a lot of iron for one fatheaded Dil Parks. Now the season was tapering off and it was time to think of heading north. The wallet was fat enough. Maybe just ease around for a month or so.

This Parks didn't know one thing about running an agency. That had been clear right from the start. On sales of the used stuff he'd been able to clip the agency regularly with one of the oldest tricks in the book. Look in all directions and say, in a low voice. "Okay, he's got a three-fifty tag on it. Personally I think that's a touch high, but I've got no authority to cut the price on it. But I like you and I think you ought to have a break. Suppose I write it up for three hundred. I'll get a hell of a chewing out, and I might lose my job. So how about twenty in cash. It saves you thirty bucks on the car. But for Christ sake don't tell anybody." Then tell Parks he had to let it go at the minimum listing of three hundred, and take the commission on that figure.

Parks didn't appreciate salesmanship.

Take that joker that came in yesterday, just looking around. Didn't want any help. Just looking. Got into conversation with him. Gave Manny the sign to go look over the sucker's car and make an estimate. Manny, on his way back through, held up seven fingers, showing that they could go to seven bills on the trade-in. Then never quote the total difference. Split it up in your head into payments.

"I got a demonstrator outside. You say you've got to pick up the wife at the beauty parlor. Okay, suppose I run you over there and drive the two of you back here. No obligation. Glad to do it. Hell, you can drive it. See how it feels."

The wife was sore. "You thinking of another car already?" she squalled.

Mooney stepped in. "He isn't thinking of a new one, ma'm. But if he was, it isn't a bad time. In another six months it'll be twice as hard to move the car you've already got, and I understand the list on this one is going up. The difference will be a lot bigger. Right now you could drive this one away for just about fifty bucks a month. You know, if you get too far behind, it's damn hard to get back to a new car. Might be up around a hundred bucks a month next year."

A little push here and a little push there. Fifty bucks a month. That didn't include the insurance, but you didn't tell them that. Plenty of time for that in a day or two. Tell them you thought they carried that separately. The payments will total about sixty-six a month, but they're happy. They're rolling on new rubber. They have their feet on a few more horses.

"Why the hell weren't you on the floor?" Parks demanded. "We had some customers in here."

"I was out selling one."

And that didn't mean anything to Parks. He wanted you handy to step on when he felt like it. He wanted to show you what a truly enormous wheel he was in this town. Address these postcards, Mooney. Here's the list. Set up that display. Run over to railway express and pick up those parts for Bernie.

He used his sleeve to wipe some fingerprints off the roof of the car he was leaning on. He didn't like to peddle this make of car. This make was like Dil Parks. All noise and flash and no guts under the hood. They were harder to move than a lot of other kinds. It was a crummy agency. No price policy. Low-pressure advertising. Maybe a sixty per cent utilization of the repair department. Sloppy, big-mouth mechanics. And Parks kept banker's hours and never knew quite what the hell was going on.

He came to with a start as he realized Dil Parks was calling him. He went over to the office door.

"You asleep out there, Mooney?"

"It's quiet enough to go to sleep."

"Hook the bike on the back end of the green demonstrator and take it out to Mrs. Parks. Tell her I'm going to be held up and I'll get a ride later to the Shermans' party and meet her there."

"How about her driving me back in? I got grease on my pants off that damn motorcycle last time."

"Damn it, Mooney, why do you always have an objection?"

Mooney knew Parks was showing off for the friend who sat in his office. Also, it had only been a token objection. To stay in key. He felt better about the whole day. He hoped the cleaning woman wouldn't be out there this time.

"Okay, okay," he muttered and turned away. Clara, the stenographer-bookkeeper, winked at him and he winked back. He rolled the three-wheeled motor scooter out of the corner of the garage and adjusted the two clamps on the back bumper of the green demonstrator. He drove the short block over to Bay Avenue and turned toward the causeway and Flamingo Key. As he drove toward the Parks home he thought it was typical of Dil Parks to own a home more pretentious than he could properly afford.

It was a house that faced the Gulf. It was in a restricted housing development on the north end of the key. To enter the development you drove through a gate which bore stern warnings about trespassing. The area was called Seascape Estates. On the very tip of the key, on the bay side, was the Seascape Yacht Club, with membership limited to the property owners within the Estates. The Parks home was three hundred yards from the Yacht Club. It was a post and beam house of cypress stained elephant gray, with touches of bright coral, wide areas of glass. The drive was of round brown pebbles rolled into asphalt. A high cypress wind fence, stained the same color as the house, provided privacy from the neighboring houses. Mooney parked the car in the circular drive, unhooked the scooter, went to the door and rang the bell. He could hear the muted double chime within the house. He rang again, but no one came. He felt a combination of irritation, anticipation and nervousness. His hands were damp.

After a few moments he walked slowly around the house. He was a man with a jerky, swaggering, belligerent walk. His face would have been nondescript except for its high order of mobility. It was a mobility thoroughly under control. He could control his expression, his tone of voice, his diction, to match his quick and instinctive appraisal of both background and character of any prospect. His was the instinctive timing of the born actor. There was, in effect, no real Mooney, no basic core of character or self-appraisal. Mooney was what the situation demanded of him, and nothing beyond that.

He stopped when he came to the rear corner of the house. In contrast to the grass in front of the house, the rear area was of raked sand. Dil's dainty little blonde wife lay in the sunlight on a maroon blanket. Her face was turned away from him. She lay face down, and above the low continual grumbling and hissing of the waves, he could hear faint music from the portable radio a foot from her blonde head. Beside her, on the blanket, was the discarded sunsuit, dark glasses, a bottle of lotion, an open book, face down. She lay nude there, toes pointed, heels a foot apart. She was warmly tanned, her tan deep except for a line across her back and her bare hips. They were tanned also, but it was a more delicate honeyed color. A low stone wall protected her from the direct view of anyone who walked down the beach. The wind fences on the side boundaries of the property protected her in those two directions.

Mooney tore a leaf from a lush plant that grew close to the house and rolled it slowly between thumb and finger, his eyes on the woman's body, noting with experienced approval the delicacy of her waist, the round firmness of the small thighs, the emphasis of the crease down her back between the shoulder blades, a crease which, as it neared the small of her back, shallowed to show the small knuckles of the vertebrae and ended at a small downy hollow before the soft rising tilt of her buttocks. This woman had baffled Mooney for over three months. His sure instincts told him she was a tramp. He had sensed her restlessness. But her weapon was a species of amused scorn.

He had donned many of his faces for her, carefully chosen one manner after another, and had awakened only wry hidden laughter. It had rubbed his ego raw. Women had always been easy, particularly this kind of woman. He could not understand continual failure. Failure created self-doubt. Looking at her there he had the first dim understanding of what drove men to rape.

Gulls tipped and cried above waves flecked brown with floating weed. Far out a white cruiser trolled. He tore another leaf from the bush, rolled it between his fingers, snapped the bruised ball of green away and smelled his fingertips. The smell was sharp, acid-sweet.

"Cough, cough," he said, just loudly enough for her to hear him.

She started violently, heels snapping together, head lifting to stare at him with sundazed eyes, sunslack face, one arm across her breasts. "Oh . . . Mooney."

"I come bearing vehicle."

"Don't just stand there."

"It's such a pleasure."

"Elderly schoolboy. This would make a nice little anecdote for Dil."

"Tell him. Let me watch you tell him. For laughs."

"At least turn your dang back, Mooney. Do that much."

"Sure." He turned around. He looked at the glass and thought of something. He moved a bit to the side to where he could see her reflection darkly in the glass. She pulled her shorts on above her knees, then lay back, her weight on her feet and the backs of her shoulders as she pulled them up over her hips. She rolled over and knelt, bending over, to hammock her breasts into the halter top. She fastened it in back and stood up and said, "Okay, Mooney." Her voice was derisive and weary.

He turned around. "Sure and I have before me a long hot ride which a cold beer would give me the strength to stand all the better."

"That phony Irish accent makes me want to fwow up."

"Tender and gentle, aren't you? Like a pricker bush."

She picked up book, glasses and lotion. "Fold the blanket, Mooney, and bring it and the radio in the house. Make sure you shake the sand off the blanket. I'll give you a beer for services rendered."

"On second thought, beer is fattening."

"All right. Bourbon."

"With just a splash of branch water, Lennie."

"Mrs. Parks, Mooney, Mr. and Mrs. Parks."

He wore a black scowl as he followed instructions. He went into the kitchen and put the blanket and radio down. He turned the radio off. She put water on top of the ice and bourbon in two tall glasses and handed him one.

"For God's sake don't try to clink glasses, Mooney. This isn't a class reunion."

"That's a bad mood you're in."

"I'm aware of it. I have troubles."

He sipped his drink. "Take me. I never have troubles. I travel light. No room in my pack for troubles. Or for houses or possessions or fat problems. When I get bored, I roll along to some other place."

"Are you getting bored here?"

"The season is over. Your husband, forgive me, rubs me the wrong way."

"You're not alone."

"But off I go. And I never see him again."

"I think I envy you."

"Maybe, Lennie, there's somebody you could be visiting. Pack a small bag. Come on along. We'll do some loafing at Myrtle Beach and then you can come back here all . . . refreshed."

"You're a cold bastard, Mooney."

"Do you mean I don't pant and sigh and promise undying love and devotion? Then you're right. I don't. I make a flat offer."

As he finished his drink he became aware that she was looking at him strangely, her head tilted a little bit to the side, her forehead slightly wrinkled.

"What's up?"

"You're cold, Mooney, and you're shrewd. Maybe you could give me an idea or two on my problem. It might mean some money for you. Maybe a lot of money."

"They call me honest Mooney."

"It would be honest, practically."

"Anything where I get a lot of money isn't going to be honest."

"It could be, you know."

"Dishonesty is risk. I don't take risks."

"No risks."

"So then pour another drink. I'll listen. What is your problem?"

She looked at him and seemed to be making up her mind about something. "Does Dil expect you right back?"

"That I can check. Where's the phone?"

"Through there, on the right."

He went in and dialed the agency. When Clara answered he thickened his voice and added a touch of cracker. She told him Mr. Parks had left for the day. He told Lennie that.

"Maybe he's coming back here."

"No. He told me to tell you he'd get a ride to the Shermans' party later on. That's why he had me bring the car out. So you can get there."

She nodded. "Then you've got a little time?"

"All the time we need."

"I'm all sticky from that lotion. I want to feel clean. You make another drink, Mooney. Make me one too and bring it on in."

He made the drinks. Just as he finished he heard the dull roar of the shower. He carried the two drinks down a hallway. The bathroom door was ajar.

"Where do you want your drink?" he yelled.

"Bring it in."

He took a deep breath and pushed the door open. It was a transparent glass shower stall. The hot water had steamed the glass. He could not see her clearly.

"Give me a sip."

She opened the glass door and put her head out. He held the glass to her lips. His hands were shaking. She smiled at him. "Ever scrub a back?"

"On special occasions."

"This is special, Mooney."

He was dubious. He felt that this was another form of torture. He suspected that she would change quickly and start laughing at him again. He told himself not to hope. He was dubious for some time. He even had faint misgivings when he carried her, dripping wet in his arms, her head nestled into the hollow of his throat, into the next room. But then the last faint doubt was gone, very thoroughly and completely erased from his mind. She had all the talent he had anticipated and more. After a long time he began to hear the surf again, and the thin harsh gull cries, and the sputtering sound of a light low-flying plane. He went to his clothes and got cigarettes on request and brought them back to the bed. At the next request he put on his shorts and shoes and went to the bathroom and got the two drinks. They needed more ice. He added more bourbon when he added ice. He took them back to the bedroom. She had put on a skirt and she was hooking her bra. Her hair was tangled and her face had the soft look of satiety. She sat on the dressing table bench and began brushing her hair as he finished dressing.

She began to talk about her problem. He listened carefully to all of it.

"I heard about the money. Those things get exaggerated, Lennie."

"Darling, this is true. It really is. But no lawyer will touch it. Uncle Paul's contacts are too good. He's too respected. They won't admit he's insane."

"And this Preston pair—they're cutting you out."

"I'm afraid so."

"I'm no lawyer."

"I know that. But you're shrewd, darling. You know people. You know how to handle people. I've thought of all kinds of wild things. Now I need ideas. I want you to have some ideas."

"What kind of an old joker is he?"

"Tall. Cold eyes. Very dignified. A culture bug. Music and books and paintings and so on. Keeps his distance. No friends. He doesn't like Dil at all. I don't know whether he likes me." She leaned toward the mirror to make up her mouth.

Mooney sat on the edge of the bed, glass in one hand, cigarette in the other, watching her. "As I get it, people think he's pretty crazy. But they like him. Like a town monument to something or other. The thing is to have him act more crazy."

"Like what?"

"It would have to be faked."

"How do you mean?"

"If he did something really off-beat, something the whole town talked about, then one of the lawyers would take it."

"I'm positive they would. One was nearly willing. I

could sense it. But not quite. Ben Piersall is the one I really want to handle it, but he wanted no part of it."

"But even Piersall would reconsider if, for example, the old doc started hearing voices, or coming to town without his pants."

"Of course, but . . ."

"We have to think of how to make him do something irrational, something he won't be able to explain."

Her face in the mirror nodded at him. "I see what you're thinking, darling. I think maybe it's pretty bright."

"It wouldn't have to be anything too startling. It could be a lot of little things. If I could hear him talk, I could imitate his voice. You could brief me on what he calls people. Hell, I could call up Flamingo Builders Supply and order fifty gallons of polka dot paint. Or I could use his voice and put a wild ad in the paper, put it in over the phone. He'll deny it. People will say he just didn't remember doing it. Hell, Lennie, in a week or two I can have the whole town saying he's really flipped. Where do I stand?"

"Would you do it?" She turned around on the bench.

"Where do I fit? What comes to me?"

"I don't know. I'd have to see if it works. I'd have to see what we get out of it."

"You said there'd be no risk. There's risk in this."

"Not very much."

"Enough to be paid for."

"I can't pay you any money. Not until afterward. I can't pay you anything."

"Not anything at all?"

Her eyes turned sly. She sat facing him. She arched her back a tiny bit, lowered her head, looked at him through her lashes. "I could be a sort of . . . sort of promissory note."

"You certainly show promise."

"Is that all, Mooney? Hey, go away. Not now, darling. There isn't time."

"Then when?"

"When do you start?"

"After you make a chance for me to hear the old coot talk."

"Tomorrow is Wednesday. Let me see. Pick me up here at ten in the morning. We'll go out there. I'll think of something. He's never refused to see me. He's just . . . cool toward me. Can you get away?"

"I'll get away."

"After we see him, we can talk about us."

"Just talk?"

"About us and a place where we can meet and plan this thing. A quiet private place. You can think about that, about such a place, and you can think of ways we can make Uncle Paul look weird. I'll try to think of some too. Where do you live, Mooney?"

"A room at the Palm Lodge. It's a little crummy, but it's near the center of town."

"Dang it, I hoped maybe you lived in one of those nice private little cabanas at South Flamingo Beach."

"I've been considering a change."

They looked at each other. Mooney could feel the pulse in his throat. "I could move today," he said.

"Get one with a phone, darling."

He left by the back door and walked around the house. The motor scooter started on the third try. He drove back down the key, squinting against the warm wind. He thought of her, all wet and silky, and his loins felt an urgency that superseded the warm sense of depletion. He found that to be entirely at ease, he had to keep thinking of her. He did not like thinking of the other thing, the old man and his craziness. Nor did he want to think of the money. There were small shrill alarms in the back of his mind that could only be stilled by thinking intently of Lennie Parks.

During his life he had cut corners in many small safe ways. But this was more than sharpshooting. Once, when he was twenty-five, he had been roughed up by a pair of cops. It had made him sick to his stomach. It was one of the memories he seldom took out and examined. This could be trouble before it was over. Maybe it would be best to forget it. He had finally had the woman. That should be enough. Pull stakes and roll. But it was much woman. Fire and ice. Too much to turn your back on, yet. Stay a while. Until it began to look too shaky, and then take off. The cabana rent would make a hole in the bankroll. With the season rolling to a stop, there wouldn't be much coming in. But the woman was worth it. Thirty-four years or so of knowledge in a young girl body. It certainly wasn't attraction or love on her part. She was trading. She was using what she had to make a deal with. It was his language, and he knew he had accepted it at its proper value. They weren't kidding each other.

He left the agency a little earlier than usual. He took his own car to South Flamingo Beach. The rental agent was still there. Six of the cabanas were empty. He picked one on the end. Cars parked by it could not be seen from either the beach or the road. It was on pilings. Heavy draperies could be drawn across the front windows. He paid a one-month rental, and took possession. He moved his stuff out of the Lodge into the cabana. He laid in a small stock of liquor. He dusted the place, rearranged the few pieces of furniture, fluffed the pillows—and ceased only when he realized that he was acting like a nervous and elderly bride. He was sardonically amused at himself.

Before he went to bed he washed out an overdue stack of socks and underwear. In the night when the wind awoke him he thought of the old man and he was frightened. But it was her price, and he would pay it, and maybe there was no risk. Maybe there was no risk at all.

CHAPTER SIX

Ronnie arrived in Flamingo on Wednesday, the thirteenth day of April. He stepped down from the silver car of the Seaboard Airline Railroad onto the open platform. He tipped the porter, picked his pigskin bag out of the lineup and moved off to one side, smelling the warmth of the air, looking at the women in their thin bright clothing.

He spotted coin lockers in the waiting room. He put his bag in one, bundled his tweed topcoat in on top of it and, after a moment of hesitation, put his brown felt hat in also before slamming the door. He bounced the key on his palm, slipped it into his side pocket and turned, whistling thinly, back out into the sunlight.

He was in his late twenties. He was slim and erect and blond and his suit sat well on him, gray gabardine hanging properly from good shoulders. He walked in a springy way and his expression was that of a man just about to smile. He had the nordic look of a ski instructor, the pale blue eyes of snow-country distances. He looked alert, intelligent and friendly.

Ronnie was in the mood of a man on vacation. He walked slowly down Bay Avenue from the station, absorbing the mood and flavor of the town. He had seldom worked in a town this small. And though he was not here to perform his practiced, specialized task, habit was strong. He mapped streets as he walked, studied traffic density, measured the timing of the traffic lights.

He had walked in just this way in many strange cities. He took infinite pains. Inattention to detail has ruined many small businesses. Ronnie was, in effect, a small business enterprise, solvent, successful. He had been on call for seven years, ever since he completed his first and only prison term at the age of twenty-one. When any syndicate underling became too greedy, or too ambitious or too unmanageable, or whenever a particularly vicious double-cross had been accomplished or was contemplated, there was a choice of specialists who could be contacted. Ronnie was one of them. The most successful one. During the seven years he had killed twelve men and two women.

There were several reasons for his continuing success. There was his capacity for planning carefully. There was his use of a variety of techniques so that no standard pattern could be ascribed to him. He did not look or act the part. On rare occasions when he had been picked up, he made no attempt to deny a criminal record. But in his quiet voice, using excellent diction and grammar, he would point out that he owned a small and profitable tire-recapping business in central Pennsylvania, and he was on a business trip. He had papers to prove it. And he did own the small business, and it was profitable.

It was in the tiny cluttered office of his small business concern that he would receive a phone call. It would come from a pay station in New York or Chicago or Kansas City or New Orleans. It would be a voice he didn't recognize. Go to Las Vegas and call such and such a number. He would make the trip. The phone call would result in a contact in a dark car or a dimly lighted room.

The instructions were simple. "Frankie Delani in Reno."

And some time during the next month one Frankie Delani would cease to live—by knife or bullet, by a wire around the throat, or a fall from a high place, or a heavy blow on the head. And Ronnie would return to Pennsylvania. Soon thereafter he would receive payment. It would come in various ways. It was always in cash, in used bills. There was never any specific clue as to who had sent it. Sometimes he suspected. But he never knew. Sometimes when the amount seemed too small, he was annoyed. Other times it would be larger, more satisfying. But only Ronnie knew that he would have performed the assigned tasks with no pay at all. Once, between assignments, he had gone to a strange city. He had selected a name at random, taking it from a phone book. It had been very simple because, in this case, the man had had no presentiment of danger. But Ronnie had made the stalk as carefully as with the others.

But he resolved he would not do that again. It had been pleasurable, but it had meant a step across a thin line. He was aware that he was not as other men. He had read enough to know that other men, if they could see inside him, would call him psychopathic. So long as he kept his wish to kill within the channel of those cases assigned to him, he could pose as a man of business and the difference would not show on the outside. But he was superstitiously afraid that were he to continue to kill without cause, he would become marked, and other men would begin to read the difference when they looked at his face.

There were, in the country, perhaps twenty men who knew his function and his importance. Few of them knew him by sight. They did not want to know him better. Should he ever fail, they did not want any tie-in provable. Some of the men who knew of him were police officials. Those men, wise and cynical in their trade, felt that he performed a reasonably valid function. Without Ronnie, and a very few other specialists, open warfare could result. A strong syndicate meant more crime—but more of a surface appearance of law and order. Weak links in the administrative chain had to be removed. It pleased Ronnie to think that two of the men who had known of him—had been high enough up in their territories to know of him—had been eliminated through his efforts.

The last time he had come to Florida, he had come on assignment. He had come to Tampa three years ago. The man was named Mendez. Mendez had been involved in a serious disagreement over control of bolita. Serious for Mendez. It had taken three weeks of planning. Mendez had a bodyguard. But he had a bad habit of walking out of a place ahead of them. Ronnie had blown Mendez' chest open with a twelve-gauge shotgun on a rainy night as the man left a bar.

This trip was different. This trip was a change in routine. A thick-set man with white hair and a thin high voice had given him the instructions in person. That, in itself, was a departure.

"You know Harry Mullin?"

"I know of him."

"Know he crashed out?"

"I read about it."

"He's got good connections. He's got something lined up. He wants a box man and a gun. He asked for the Ace for the box. You're the gun."

"It's not my line."

"It was your line once."

"It didn't work out."

"You're going into it again, one more time."

"Okay. Why the pressure?"

"No pressure. What we know about what Mullin has lined up, it sounds sour. Anyway, the word is that it has to go sour, not for Mullin but for the Ace. The Ace got loose too easy. Nobody wondered too much about it. Now we know."

"He made a little trade?"

"A couple of little trades. We just bought us a new assistant D.A. out there, and he had the word on it. It would be hard to pick off the Ace, as a straight deal. So it goes this way. You go in on it as the gun. Let the Ace do the box work before you take him. Don't tip Mullin in advance because he's nervous. You can tell him afterward, if you have to."

"I'd like it better if it was both of them."

"Nobody has anything against Mullin."

"Has anybody got anything for him, particularly?"

"I see what you mean, kid. But don't get ape sweat. Mullin is nervous, but they couldn't jar anything out of him."

"If I decide to make it both, would there be a big kickback?"

"Not too much. Riverio might yelp, but not loud. Riverio thought the gun ought to come out of another area, and that gives us the chance to use you."

"Does Mullin know I'm in?"

"And the Ace does too."

"No squawk?"

"Nothing I heard of. It's a place called Flamingo, Florida. On the west coast. Get down there by April 12th or 13th. Check the book in the Chamber of Commerce. There'll be a message there for you."

"What's their deal?"

"All I know is Riverio said it sounded sour to him. It could even be a bank. Mullin likes banks."

"If it's a bank, I'll take both of them before it starts."

"Use your judgment."

"I don't want any part of banks."

"They'll be strangers in town, and keeping their heads down, so it ought to be easy."

"Don't pay me like it was easy."

"It will be fat pay."

"Won't the Ace be jumpy?"

"He's been loose for two years. He's stopped worrying by now. You better wait and see how they plan to score. It might be a good thing. You might make out."

"No banks."

"Then it would probably have to be both."

"Mullin is pretty heavy right now."

"There's that, too. But he's smart enough to stay off the streets."

"I haven't seen the Ace in five years. We didn't get along."

"Doesn't that make it easier?"

"Maybe."

Ronnie opened the car door and got out. The car drove away. Ronnie watched the tail-lights through light snow, until the car turned a corner. Then he turned his overcoat collar up and started walking the ten blocks to the Broad Street Station in Philadelphia.

Now he walked down Bay Avenue in Flamingo in holiday mood. This one pleased him. He was glad it had worked out this way. It would be a special treat to be with the Ace and Mullin, knowing he was going to take both of them. He'd known he was going to take the pair of them as soon as it had been explained to him. Maybe they knew it too, the ones who decided policy. Taking both would be the safe way in the long run. Safer than any chance of being seen with Mullin. It would be nice to sit and chat and eat together and drink together and smile and tell stories and know every minute that those were their last few hours on earth. They wouldn't know it. They'd feel safe with him.

He remembered the first of the two women. It had been just like that. Some drinks together, and some laughs together, with him knowing all the time, every second of every minute. Watching her eyes and the way she moved her hands, and knowing all about it—knowing something she didn't know. It gave him a funny excited feeling to watch her and touch her and know she was going to end —click—like you turn off a light. He remembered how when the time was right he had put on the yellow knit gloves and hit her sharply and suddenly, and used her boyfriend's neckties to lash her wrists and ankles and then, changing the plan a little, had waited until she woke up before taking hold of her throat with his hands in the yellow gloves. It hadn't lasted very long, but it lasted longer than a knife and much longer than a bullet. Then he had left the way he had come in. Out the window to the shed roof and off the roof to the side yard, and out through the back and down the alley to the next street and down the street to the lot where he had parked the car he had rented a hundred miles away.

He walked down Bay Avenue until finally he saw, coming toward him, a girl who was sufficiently pretty. He stopped her and smiled and said, "I beg your pardon. Could you tell me where the Chamber of Commerce is?"

"It's right down at the foot of this street, just to the left when you get to the causeway."

He looked into her eyes until she looked away nervously. "Thank you very much."

She tried to edge by him. "That's all right," she said.

"Can I buy you a drink for being polite to a stranger?"

"No. No thanks. Really. I've got to run."

He let her go. He turned and watched her. She walked quickly and when she was forty feet away she looked back and saw him standing there, still smiling. She ducked her head and hurried along, clutching her parcels. Ronnie chuckled and turned and went on his way.

The girl behind the desk in the Chamber of Commerce pointed toward the big open notebook and said, "They leave the messages in there—alphabetical."

He moved down the counter to the notebook and looked under R. Only a very few in the business knew the full name he used in the tire business, Ronald Crown. No one knew the name he had been born with, Ronald Dearlove. It was his name that had given him his first acquaintance with the law, and with himself. Goaded beyond reason by schoolyard taunts, he had beaten an eight-year-old contemporary into unconsciousness with a short length of pipe. He kept striking after the other boy was down. Wild anger changed by slow degrees into hot rising pleasure. The other child was four months in the hospital. For a time it was thought he would not recover.

He found the message under R. *Dear Ronnie—While you're in town give us a ring at 4-6040*. It was signed "Alice." The *li* part of the name was written faintly, the *Ace* bold and black. He thought it a typical example of Ace's childishness.

He walked back up Bay Avenue and phoned from a drugstore booth.

A man answered, saying, "Hello?"

"Ronnie speaking."

"Where are you calling from?"

"A drugstore booth."

"Be at the corner of Bay Avenue and Palm at eight tonight. The southeast corner. The Ace will pick you up. Gray Buick, three beeps on the horn." The man hung up. Ronnie shrugged and hung up. He stood in the doorway of the drugstore. Young girls walked by in shorts and halters. Heavy women in print dresses. Men in slacks and sandals and T-shirts. Sun was bright on the street, blazing from chrome trim. New traffic lines were bright yellow against the gray blue of the asphalt.

He sensed that Flamingo was too small to permit complete freedom of motion. Strangers would be noted and remembered. He had a drugstore sandwich and walked down to a small city park and sat on a bench and watched the traffic and the blue bay water and the cars heading out across the causeway to Flamingo Key. People fished from the bridge. A mother and child stood by the sea wall and fed bread to the gulls. He could hear the child laugh.

He walked back and located the corner where he would be picked up. He spent the rest of the day in the movies.

At ten fifteen on Wednesday morning, Mooney was sitting beside Lennie Parks as she drove down the narrow street toward Dr. Tomlin's stone house. He felt nervous and irritable. Lennie, in a pale blue blouse and white skirt, was calm, casual, impersonal.

"You sure this won't seem funny?" he asked.

"Not in the least."

The big iron gates were closed. Lennie parked the car beyond the gates and they got out. She pushed the bell button set into the gate post. They saw Arnold Addams coming down from the house, wearing a white jacket.

"Good morning, Mrs. Parks," he said as he unlocked the gate.

"Good morning, Arnold. Is Uncle Paul around?"

"He having coffee with Miss Laurie out on the back terrace. You can go right on around, I guess."

Mooney followed her closely as they went around the house. A tall severe-looking old man sat at a shaded table with a sturdy, pretty girl. They both looked up as Mooney and Lennie approached. Mooney decided the old man looked very unfriendly. The girl got up quickly and the old man got up with the slow stiffness of age.

"Hello, Uncle Paul. Hello, Laurie," Lennie said brightly

and cheerfully. "This is Mr. Mooney. Doctor Tomlin, Mrs. Preston."

The doctor's hand had a cool papery feel.

Mooney paid particular attention to the doctor's voice. It was slow and deep, the words carefully enunciated. There was a slight quaver of age.

"That coffee looks good," Lennie said disarmingly.

"I'll bring some," the girl said and hurried off.

"Please sit down," the doctor said, no warmth in his voice. They sat at the table with him. Lennie took her cigarettes from her purse.

"Mr. Mooney works for Dil," Lennie said. "I've borrowed him today. I'm afraid this is very boring for him, carting me around. I'm soliciting contributions for the Community Concert series."

"And you've come to me, Lenora?" There was an undercurrent of sour amusement in the old man's voice.

"I know how you feel about such things, Uncle Paul, but there's no harm in trying, is there?"

"Just a waste of time and motion."

Lennie made a face. "So all I get is coffee."

Laurie Preston brought cups and saucers and a fresh pot of coffee. Mooney wanted to hear the old man talk some more. "Lovely grounds you have here inside your wall, sir."

"Give credit to Laurie. She has the touch. Lenora said you work for Dillon?"

"I sell cars for him."

"I imagine you are an excellent salesman."

"I've done it for quite a few years. Why would you think I'd be a good salesman?"

"You carry yourself so confidently. And you seem to be observant."

Mooney felt more at ease. "Observant enough, sir, to see the front end of that car in the garage. The old black Packard. What is it? Nineteen thirty-nine?"

"Thirty-eight. It's been a little over a hundred and twenty thousand miles."

"We couldn't give you much on a trade, Doctor. But don't you think it's about time?"

"I have no intention of trading it. None whatsoever," the old man said coldly.

Mooney smiled. "As Mrs. Parks just said, no harm in trying."

Laurie and Lenora made light conversation in the manner of two women who barely know each other and do not care for each other. Soon the coffee was finished and they left. Arnold let them back out the gate. They got into the car and Lennie drove away.

"That old gent is crazy like a fox."

"He ought to be put away."

"Who are you trying to kid, Lennie?"

"He's taken those Prestons in. Who are they? You should see Joe Preston. A complete nothing."

"The girl seems nice."

"If you go for that type. She's a peasant. They're a pair of adventurers. I can't understand why he took them in. He isn't competent to protect himself from a pair like that."

"Maybe he was lonesome."

"He wasn't lonesome when we offered to move in with him."

"Maybe you and Dil aren't the type."

"Don't try to be witty. If that's what you're trying to be."

"Calm down, will you?"

"I'm calm. Get one thing firmly in mind, Mooney. I'm not interested in your opinion of him. I want to know if you can do what we talked about."

"I'll practice some. You can check me on it after I give it a workout. It shouldn't be too tough."

"Let's hear you right now."

" 'I have no intention of trading it. None whatsoever.' "

"Hmmm. Not bad. Not very good, either."

" 'I have no intention of trading it, Lenora. None whatsoever.' "

"That's better, Mooney."

"We'll check it over the phone. That's where it has to sound right. Don't worry, I'll get it down pat."

"When?"

"Hell, I don't know."

"Today?"

"I have to go back to work. When I get a chance I'll call you from the shop. You be home?"

"Call me about three."

"I . . . I moved into one of the cabanas. The end one, on the south."

He watched her face and it did not change. "How nice for you."

"It's not bad there."

She said nothing further. He felt frustrated. He didn't know how he had annoyed her. She let him out without a word. He stalked toward the agency car he had left on the downtown street. Just as he touched the doorhandle, she said, "Mooney!"

He turned around and looked at her. She was leaning across the front seat. "Well, come here!" she said impatiently.

He walked back to the car, scowling.

"Don't sulk, darling," she said.

"What do you expect me to . . ."

"Hush now. No tantrums, doll baby. Is there a phone in your cabana?"

"Yes, there is."

"Then why don't you call me there?"

His mood of depression was gone, all at once. "Sure thing! I'd be glad to . . ."

"Stop glowing and give me the key then."

He took the key off his ring and handed it to her. She winked at him and said, "If it's a good imitation, darling, I'll wait there for you and we'll celebrate. If it isn't any good, I'll be gone before you can get back. Understand?"

"That isn't fair, damn it. How can I . . ."

But she had put the car in gear and she was gone. He

looked after the car and then went and got in the agency car, slammed the door and raced the motor.

All the way back to the agency he practiced the timbre and cadence of Paul Tomlin's voice.

CHAPTER SEVEN

Laurie noticed that after Lenora Parks and Mr. Mooney had left, Doctor Paul seemed troubled.

"She's very pretty," Laurie said.

"Eh? Oh, Lenora. Yes, she's pretty enough. Dresden type. Pretty and restless and greedy."

"Is something bothering you, Doctor Paul?"

"Nothing, Laurie. Nothing important. I just keep wondering what was on her mind. She's never done anything in her life without a purpose. I just don't know why she came here. I've made it clear to them that if they want to see me, either of them, or both of them, they should call first. I'm quite aware that the knowledge of the money I keep here is a source of acute, almost physical anguish to Lenora. I know that I am the reason she married Dillon. She must be a badly frustrated woman. She must be very distressed at my . . . durability. And very upset about your living here with me."

"Upset?"

"Don't be so unworldly, Laurie. She hates you. That was quite obvious to me, the first time she met you. I hope she isn't planning to hurt you in any way."

"How could she hurt me?"

"I don't know. She might try to discredit you with me. I don't see how she would go about that, though. If there is any weak link here, it would be Joe. She might try to hurt you through Joe."

"Are you certain you aren't imagining this?"

"I don't think so. I'd like to know where that man fits in. Mooney. That was his name, wasn't it?"

"That's right."

"Not a very good type, Laurie. He has the look and flavor of an opportunist. He was more on edge than he should have been on a routine call like that. Those two are plotting something."

She touched the back of his hand. "They can't hurt anything, Doctor Paul. There isn't anything they can do. And I think you're imagining things."

He smiled. "I hope you're right, my dear."

"You've acted a little odd lately."

"Have I? Let me tell you something, Laurie. These last few months have been happy months. I didn't know I would ever feel this alive again. It could be that I'm superstitious about it. The last time I was completely happy, the world fell apart. That could be the reason for the presentiment of evil. Contentment is a gift horse. I have the feeling that something bad is going to happen. I don't know what it is. I don't know which door to guard. Maybe you'd like to take my mind off it."

"Who will it be this morning?"

"Let me see. Something new for you and old for me. Some Conrad, I think. I think you might like him. He's on the next to the top shelf, near the windows. Find the volume that has 'Typhoon' in it. You'll like the captain, I'm sure."

She took the cups in and left him sitting there. She went to the library and hunted for the book he wanted. He enjoyed having her read to him. Reading seemed to give him headaches lately. She knew that he enjoyed listening and at the same time watching her discover something new. She was learning to read much better, and did not stumble over words nearly as often as in the beginning. It pleased her to read to him. It made her feel as though she was in that way earning a portion of the money he paid her each Friday. But it seemed wrong to enjoy it as much as she did. She tried to talk to Joe about what was in the books. Joe would listen for a time, contemptuously amused, and would soon lose patience.

"Books, books. What's in books, kid? What's got you so all wound up anyhow?"

"Joe, honey, you don't understand what . . ."

"Digging around in those books all the time. They're

not for you and me, sugar. That's not living. Here, I'll show you what living is."

"Joe, honey, stop. Wait a minute. Let me explain to you."

"What is there to explain? Hell, the old boy likes his books. You get along with him real good. That's fine. But don't try to drag me in on it. If you want me entertained, why don't you get the old boy to put a TV set here in our bedroom. That's the way you keep up with the world, sugar. That's the way you know what's going on. Not out of those old books. Living is something like this. And this."

"Joe . . . please."

"And like this too. Isn't this being alive? Isn't it?"

"Oh, Joe. Yes, honey. Oh, yes, yes, yes."

She found the right Conrad book. She walked slowly back through the house toward the garden. She frowned as she thought of Joe. Steadily and inevitably she was growing away from him. She wondered if Doctor Paul knew that. She and Joe had less and less to talk about. Now his conversation seemed curiously empty. Like shallow water where you can see every stone on the bottom. Doctor Paul's conversation was like a deep pool. You could not see bottom. You could look down into the pool and see the deep shifting of green shadows, of things partially understood. Doctor Paul's mind was like some of the passages in the books. It could mean one thing and a lot of other things too, and each time you read it you would see something you missed before.

Lately, when Joe talked to her, she could nod and say the right things without even hearing him. ". . . bought me a beer when he found out I was a Giant fan . . . watched those kids water skiing near the municipal pier . . . must have been a heart attack or something, because they took her away in an ambulance . . . he says to me . . . so I said listen bud you're talking to a guy who really knows California . . . so he says . . . and brother I told him off . . . she was driving a bright red Thunderbird

. . . so then I told him the oldie about the plumber and the night nurse . . ."

She knew that her horizons had been the same. But the world had grown larger for her. On this morning, reading to Doctor Paul from this book she had never heard of, the world would grow larger still, and Joe would be left a little farther behind. The only close remaining element of their marriage was the physical. And she knew that her recent heightened interest in the physical was probably a reaction to the loss of the other elements of their marriage. Joe was pleased with her responsiveness. She could not tell him that she now feared for even that aspect, because she had lately begun to feel a vague distaste for the way he looked. His sideburns had begun to look absurd. His over-long fingernails looked cheap and affected. She was distressed by the spots of acne near his lips. That had never bothered her before. She was offended by the oil marks his hair left on their pillows. She resented picking up his dirty shorts and socks, washing his comb, replacing the top on the toothpaste, picking black hairs out of the sink.

She was afraid that soon everything would be gone, and she did not know what she would do without him.

She walked into the garden. Doctor Paul filled his pipe. She opened the book to "Typhoon." Her voice was clear, distinct, childlike, in the soft April garden. " 'Captain MacWhirr of the steamer Nan-Shan, had a physiognomy that, in the order of material appearances, was the exact counterpart of his mind: it presented no marked characteristics of firmness or stupidity; it had no pronounced characteristics whatever; it was simply ordinary, irresponsive and unruffled.' "

Toby Piersall, at eleven, was brown and thin and agile, with a head that looked too large for him. But there was in his face a promise that he would look very much like his father, Ben. And, barring any serious psychological hurt, he might become a man very like Ben—large, mild, steady, purposeful—with oblique and surprising humor, with an outsize capacity for both love and loyalty.

He was in his second term of junior high. His last class of the day was American History. He sat at the fourth desk from the front in the row by the windows. Mr. Weed was talking about Wilson and the League of Nations. Toby wore an attentive look, but he was not hearing a word. He could see Mr. Weed's mouth moving, but he had achieved that state of hypnosis where the room seemed entirely silent. Mr. Weed was like a television commercial with the sound turned off.

Toby Piersall was thinking of the sheet he had torn out of a magazine. It was in his notebook, on the slanted top of the desk in front of him. He had come across it during some forbidden reading. Magazines that concerned themselves with true crime cases were not on the official Toby Piersall reading list. The penalty for possession of such magazines was drastic. He would be grounded. No bike for a week. But he had a friend named Carl Gruen who was not similarly restricted. Carl had a playroom which adjoined the family garage. Carl was a true crime addict. The magazines were stacked high there. When Carl was short of money he had a nasty habit of charging a reading fee, but usually he was generous.

Toby Piersall turned back the sheets of his notebook until he could see the clipping. It showed a man in full face and in profile. There was a number on a placard that was hung around his neck.

He read once again what it said underneath. "Harry Mollinetti, alias Harry Mullin, alias Harold Moon. Escaped in January from state prison where he was serving consecutive sentences for bank robbery, second degree murder and kidnapping. This man is the most recent addition to the F.B.I.'s 'ten most wanted' list. Warning: He is probably armed and may be considered very dangerous. If you see this man, report to the nearest police station immediately."

Toby studied the face again. The man who had roared at him on the Mather dock looked older and thinner. But it *did* look a little like the same man. He read the physical description again. "Height, five feet ten and a half. Weight 172. Hair: Dark. Complexion: Swarthy. Distinguishing marks or characteristics: Two bullet scars on back of left shoulder. Triangular scar on top of left wrist."

Toby put the clipping out of sight. He was troubled. It was hard to relate this sort of man with the quiet bayfront neighborhood he knew so well. Toby did not want to make a fool of himself. He did not want to cry wolf. But he could not put the possibility out of his mind.

The last class of the day ended. He walked slowly back to his home room. At dismissal, he went out to the racks and piled his books in his bike basket. He and Dub Rowls rode home through the afternoon sunshine. Dub lived a few houses away.

"You sore about something?" Dub asked.

"Just thinking about something."

"What are you thinking about?"

"Nothing much."

"I'm going to take the boat out. Want to come?"

"I guess not."

"You sick or something?"

"I told you I'm thinking about something."

"Then have yourself a good time thinking." Dub speeded up and rode on ahead. Toby kept the same pace. He wondered if he should have let Dub in on it. Not yet. It was still his problem. There was obviously one thing to do. Watch the man next door. Try to get a good look at him. Sneak over there at night and try to look through the windows. Try to see the back of the man's left shoulder. Try to get a look at his wrist. That would be proof. With proof, there wouldn't be anybody who could laugh at him. And there would be no punishment for reading those magazines.

Mooney was happy that Dil Parks had picked this day to stay off his back. Dil was obviously too worried and upset to bully the help. Mooney wondered how bad the trouble was. Maybe Dil was about to lose his franchise.

It wouldn't be surprising. The regional inspector who had been around a month ago had looked as though he smelled something bad. The shop was dirty. The records were messed up. The parts inventory was in bad shape.

Mooney spent an hour in the sun in the lot, irritable and impatient while a Negro stood and stared in silent communion with an elderly two-hundred-dollar Buick. From time to time he would kick a tire gingerly. When he left he said he would be back. Mooney, in a low voice, practiced the sound of Dr. Tomlin's voice. At five minutes of three he crossed from the agency to a hardware store diagonally down the street. He shut himself in the phone booth in the back and called the cabana.

Lennie's low cautious voice said, "Yes?"

"Lenora, I would like to know why you brought that man to my home. What is your relationship with him?"

"Good God!" she said softly.

"I do not like to hear a young woman use that kind of language, Lenora."

"Stop it, Mooney."

"Is it any good?"

"It's almost too good. It gave me a funny feeling. It made me feel shivery."

"Will you stay there?"

"How long?"

"I could leave for good in about an hour. Or leave now and come back."

"Leave now," she said.

He did not go back inside. He took his own car from behind the agency and drove to the cabana. The blue demonstrator was hidden in the concealed drive. He went up the steps and went in. She turned from the window when she heard him. She was a dark silhouette against the bright afternoon glare of the Gulf. He went to her to take her in his arms, but she disengaged herself firmly.

"I want to talk to you, Mooney."

"Want a drink?"

"Yes, thanks. You did that a lot better than I thought

you would. Go ahead, make the drinks while I talk. I've been thinking that we could start it right now."

"So quick?"

"What's the point in waiting? It will be done sooner. You would have fooled me completely with that imitation. You could fool other people right now. You could make the first call right now. I want you to."

He took her drink to her. She sat on the studio bed with it in her hand. "Okay," he said without enthusiasm.

"There's a realtor in town who does a lot of talking. He'd spread the word quickly. Uncle Paul used to deal with him a lot, after Dil's father died. His name is Bud Hedges, and Uncle Paul calls him Benjamin. Now let's go over this very carefully, Mooney. I want it to be perfect."

"Let's go," he said. And he sat and listened to her, sat close beside her. When he tried to touch her she moved away and became angry for a moment.

"Benjamin? This is Doctor Tomlin speaking."

"Hello there, Doctor! I thought I recognized your voice. I hope you're putting something on the market."

"Not today, Benjamin. I would like you to look around, quietly you understand, and see if you can pick something up for me."

"Certainly, Doctor! It's a pleasure. It will be nice to work together again."

"Here is what I am looking for, Benjamin. About two or three thousand feet of key, Gulf to bay. Sand beach. Would you have any ideas about that?"

Mooney held the phone, the woman's head close to his. She was biting her lip. Hedges said, "I think that could be done. We'll have to go quite a way south. Down around Marco, maybe around the Hurricane Pass area south of Naples."

"You don't seem to understand, Benjamin. I want that land on Flamingo Key."

Mooney heard the man gasp. "On Flamingo Key! Doctor, that's heavily built up."

"Just a few fishing shacks, Benjamin."

The man laughed nervously. "Fishing shacks? You mean deluxe motels and beach apartment buildings, don't you?"

"Very astute, Benjamin. That's what we'll have out there some day when the causeway is built. I have reliable information that it is going to be built and soon. Now is the time to buy that land."

"But, Doctor, the causeway has . . ."

"If you can't handle this, Benjamin, I can find someone else who will be glad to handle it. Joe Logan for example."

"Joe has been dead for . . ."

"Find that land for me, Benjamin, and make certain the title is clear and find out how much it will cost me, then phone me back. Be very quiet about this."

"Yes, Doctor. I'll surely do that, Doctor," Hedges said in that reassuring tone used with invalids and small children.

Mooney hung the phone up carefully. Lennie squeezed his arm. Her eyes were dancing. "It was plain lovely," she said. "That will give him a story he can tell all over town. Poor old Doctor Tomlin has forgotten the causeway was built years ago. Bud is the type who will go all over town asking what he should do. By tomorrow everybody will know about it and be talking about it. That Joe Logan touch was absolutely perfect. I'm glad I remembered about Joe."

"He seemed to swallow it."

"Now here's the next call, Mooney. There's a man named . . ."

"Slow down, Lennie."

"What do you mean?"

"I made a call. You wanted me to make a call. I made it. Isn't that easy to understand? Tomorrow I'll make another one."

She looked into his eyes. Her smile was crooked. "Driving a hard bargain?"

"Could be."

She ran her fingertips down his cheek. "Pull the drapes across, darling. And lock the door."

Gulf glare came through the draperies and filled the room with muted gold. Afterward it made tawny highlights on her flesh as he lay and watched her dress. When she was dressed she sat on the edge of the bed, took the cigarette from his lips, inhaled, put the cigarette back between his lips and sighed deeply.

"Tomorrow?" he asked.

"You have a job, don't you?"

"I keep telling myself."

"I have to be careful too, you know."

"I know that. But you want the calls made, too."

"Yes, I want the calls made."

"Three o'clock?"

"I guess so, Mooney, I guess so. And from here I'll have to go to a tea."

"Suppose there weren't any calls to be made, Lennie?"

"Then I wouldn't be here."

"Are you that cold a proposition?"

"Don't let 'ums pride be hurt, baby doll."

"Well, hell!"

"Just teasing. After yesterday, yes, Mooney. I think I would have risked it. You're good to me. But with the phone calls, that's two birds with one rock, isn't it?"

"I guess so."

"And so there's two reasons for taking the risk. This is a small place, Mooney. And I'm watched closer than most. You can understand that."

"Sure."

She ruffled his hair quickly and left. He did not see her to the door. He heard the motor start and the car drive away. He made himself a drink. When it was half gone, he took a quick shower and dressed again. He was back at the agency by twenty-five after four.

Dil Parks saw Mooney come in. Dil felt a vague irritation with Mooney. The man seemed to be spending damn little time on the job lately. But he was not sufficiently incensed to go out onto the floor and peel his hide. He had more important things to worry about. Two weeks before, Dillon Parks had played desperate high-stakes poker with five other local men. They had played in a private room at a downtown hotel. It was a group which met regularly. Dil was not a steady member of the group. Each time he played he seemed to get burned.

But this time need had been greater than caution. He had played for the money with which to pay unpaid bills. He knew he was playing with scared money. But he could think of no other way to get what he needed. His borrowing power was exhausted. There was a maximum loan on his house, and on the agency.

One poker hand in the middle of the evening ruined him. He had played on, knowing he had no chance to recoup. He had played on, numbly, trying to understand why this ultimate catastrophe had happened to him.

It had been a five-card draw hand. Dil had been dealt three sevens, an ace and a four. He had opened. It was a pot-limit game, no limit on raises. Three men had stayed. Dil discarded the four and drew one card. He did not look at the draw. There were two other one-card draws and one two-card draw. He had intended to bet before looking, but as his opener had been raised twice and the pot was getting heavy, he spread his cards and saw the fourth seven.

His heart beat faster. This could be the big one. He hoped everybody had improved. He wanted eager play. He wanted a heavy pot. He bet heavily, but not too heavily. He was raised and he raised back. One man folded. Three of them were left in the pot. He raised heavily again. And was raised back. The three of them had begun to perspire. Marty Allen, after long thought and with great reluctance, folded his hand and said, "Too steep for me, boys. I can't even afford to protect my investment."

Dil Parks and Jim Stauch were left. Stauch was about sixty, a fat small red-faced man with poached eyes and a great deal of money. He owned bits and pieces of nearly a dozen small profitable businesses. He was originally from Georgia. He was known to be shrewd in a business deal. He was a merciless poker player. He was not a quiet poker player. He chattered all the time.

"Well now, ole Dil has got himself something he's mighty proud of, but by God, I like the look of this stuff right here, so I think I'll shove out all the rest of these chips and maybe put a check right on top of the pile. So give me just a second to write this out, Dil, and here it is, right on top of the pile, a little one and three zeros to make it look important, and with the chips and all that adds up to a little bump of let me see around about twelve hundred, yes, exactly twelve hundred."

Dil wrote out a check for two thousand, raising Stauch eight hundred. His hand was shaking so badly, the signature didn't look right. He felt as if he was dreaming it all. Stauch had taken a one-card draw, also. Dil knew that his personal balance was down below three hundred dollars. He kept his thumb over the total on the stub when he wrote out the check. Up until writing the check he had believed that his hand was the best hand. But now the worms of doubt touched the edge of his mind. Stauch seemed to be betting more heavily than a full house would warrant, had he drawn to two pair. And much more heavily than a flush. It was incredible that he could have filled a straight flush. It began to look more and more like fours. But how big? A seven was almost in the middle.

Stauch said, "Whee, this Parks is just as proud as can be. He's really got himself something. Well, I think this has gone on long enough. I think I'll just call that eight hundred and maybe give it one more little bump. About another fifteen hundred, and that makes another piece of paper for the pile. Man could run right through his checkbook in this kind of game."

Dil had felt jubilant when Stauch had indicated his desire to call, but when he added the raise to it, his heart sank. It had to be fours. Maybe good fours.

"I'll call," he said huskily. He wrote out a check for fifteen hundred and put it on the table.

Stauch said, "Well that sort of leaves it up to me to show the power and break your heart, Dil. I got me two pair here. Here's one of them." He turned over the pair of tens. "And here's the other pair." He turned over the second pair of tens. "Got 'em dealt to me cold and took a chance on passing them, seeing as how I was right under the gun, and figured I'd better draw a card I couldn't use than stand pat on the four tens. What's that over there, Dil? Four sevens? Now if that isn't a stick with a dirty end, I never did see one. What was it you folded there, Marty?"

"Full house," Marty said miserably. "Queens full of threes."

This was no longer a dream. This was nightmare. As Stauch started to pull the pot in, Dil reached over quickly and took his two checks.

"What's up?" Stauch asked, his voice much sharper.

"I just thought I'd consolidate these into one," Dil said. The room which had grown very still became noisy again as Marty started to deal a new hand.

"Sure. You do that," Stauch said.

Dil made out the check for thirty-five hundred. He made it out all except the date. As casually as he could, he said, "Jim, I'll have to transfer more cash into this account. You mind if I date this a week ahead?"

Again the room was still. After a few moments Stauch said, "That'll be okay, Dil."

Dil wrote another check for two hundred worth of chips. He played automatically. He won about a hundred and fifty dollars. At the end of the evening he cashed up and got his check for two hundred back and found that he was out three hundred and fifty of the five hundred he had started with, plus the thirty-five hundred check. Thirty-eight hundred and fifty dollars loser. In the history of the game others had lost more in one evening, but not a great deal more. Dil had never lost more than four hundred before. When the game broke up the others told him, a little too jovially, that he'd had one of those nights.

That heavy loss had changed his whole idea of himself. He had always been an optimistic man. Nothing had ever worked out very well for him, but he had never ceased to feel that sooner or later he would hit something that would pay off very well. The optimism was seriously shaken. He could not think beyond the thirty-five hundred dollar check. He knew he could not meet it. He knew he had no way of meeting it. He told himself that good old Jim Stauch would understand, and give him a break. Stauch would tear the check up and say, "You pay me when you get the chance, Dil."

But it wasn't going to be that way. He had the uneasy feeling that Jim Stauch knew the exact state of his finances, and had known even as the checks were being written that there was no money behind them.

He phoned Jim the day before the check could be presented for payment. "Jim? Dil Parks. Jim, I want to talk about that check."

"What check, Dil?"

"The check I gave you when we played poker."

"Oh, that check. What do you want to say about it?"

"I'd appreciate it, Jim, if you'd give me one more week on that. You know I'm good for it. . . . Jim, are you still there?"

"I'm still here. You want another week."

"That's right, Jim."

"Then I guess that's the way it has to be. One more week, Dil. I'll hold it for another week if that's the way you want it."

He had had odd thoughts during the week, thoughts that were not like him. After all, it was a gambling debt. Could Stauch force collection? Maybe it was time to go away. Just get in the car and go. He sat at his desk and he could hear his heart thump. Too much weight. Bad load on the heart. Too much drinking. Things weren't supposed to end this way. Not a fat man of almost forty sitting at a desk and listening to his own heart. He wished he could stop thinking that it was some kind of end, some sort of finish. Things would go on as always. They had to go on. Things just didn't stop. A check was a piece of paper. A piece of paper couldn't put an end to all the golden dreams. Lennie was no good. She didn't understand how things could be. She got impatient if you tried to talk about money and cutting down.

He sat at his desk waiting for Jim Stauch. Stauch hadn't wanted to talk about the check over the phone. He said he'd stop by. Dil wanted to get up and leave. Stauch would wait around and then leave. But that wasn't the way.

When he looked up, Stauch was standing in the doorway. It wasn't the genial talkative Jim Stauch of the poker table, of the fish fry, of the Elks Club. This was a Mr. Stauch with an unsmiling face.

"Come right on in and sit down, Jim," Dil said heartily.

Stauch came in and sat down. He put his hat on the corner of the desk. He bit the end of a cigar and spat the shred of tobacco into a corner in the general direction of the waste basket.

"You can't cover that check." It was statement, not question.

"I can, but it's a matter of time."

"I put checks in that pot. If you'd won you'd have cleared them the next morning. They were as good as cash. I won them back and tore them up, but they were as good as cash. I guess you know that."

"Yes, I know that."

"If you'd had the guts to put an IOU in the pot, it would have been up to me as to whether I wanted to gamble on accepting them. In effect those checks of yours were IOU's. But I didn't know that. I thought they were as good as my checks."

"I'm sorry about that, Jim."

"I don't give a damn whether you're glad or sorry. I don't like to be taken. I gamble for money. You lied your way into that pot and you lost. If you'd won, I'd never have known the difference. You're a born liar, Parks. You're incompetent. You aren't worth a God damn."

"Don't talk to me like that."

"I'll talk to you any way I feel like talking to you because I bought you. I bought you for thirty-five hundred bucks. Until I get that money, I own you. When do I get it?"

"I told you it's just a matter . . ."

"Of time. Maybe years. Sure. All right, Parks. How much is the mortgage on your home?"

"Around twenty-two thousand."

"You can't borrow any more on it. I checked this automobile agency. You haven't got much equity in it, and the franchise isn't worth much. How about jewelry? Your wife got much?"

"No."

"Then it's going to have to be the house. It's on good land. It ought to go for about thirty-five thousand."

"More than that."

"If we wait a year, maybe. We'll ask forty and take thirty-five. After you pay me my thirty-five hundred and pay the real estate cut of seventeen fifty, you'll have about eight clear. You can put that out as a down payment on a place that'll fit your income better than the house you have now does. There's only two of you. If you're smart you'll pick out some little place you can pick up for about nine or ten thousand. It'll cut your living expenses."

"Are you serious?"

"I'm the most serious man you ever met, Parks."

"I can't get rid of the house. What will I tell Lenora?"

"Tell her you lost it in a poker game. You should have told her already. Didn't you have guts enough to tell her?"

"I don't think you can force me to sell my house to collect on a gambling debt."

Stauch leaned back. "I was waiting for that. This isn't a gambling debt. It's a bad check. I can sue you and take your house if I have to. But I don't like suits. I can do a hell of a lot of things to you, Parks. I can get this crummy franchise lifted. I can get the bank to bear down on you. I've got weight in this town, and I don't like to use it unless I have to."

"But there's my uncle. He . . ."

"He's a rich man. I know that. And he doesn't think you're worth a damn."

"He's an old man."

"And he probably won't leave you a dime. I'm not interested in contingencies. I want cash. Pick up that phone and call any real estate agent you want. I want to hear you list that house, Parks."

"Now?"

"Right now."

"Can't you give me a week?"

"Why? Why should I?"

"Why don't you let me give you another check? For a little more? It would be just as good as the one you have. I mean, the money would still be there, in the house, for a bigger check. I could make it for thirty-six hundred. Thirty-seven?"

"Make it a nice round four thousand, Parks."

"Five hundred dollars for another week?"

"I'll give you a break. I'll make it two weeks. Two weeks from today."

"That's a lot of money."

"Not as much as thirty-five hundred you don't have. Write it out. No, damn it. How stupid do you think I am? Don't write it on the agency account."

"I wasn't thinking," Dil said humbly.

He wrote a check for four thousand on his personal account, dating it two weeks ahead. Stauch gave him the old check. Stauch turned in the doorway and said, "If you didn't have the money you should have stayed away from that game, Parks."

Long after he had gone, Dil tore up the old check. Two weeks. What could he do in two weeks? He thought of the old man and the money the old man kept in the big safe. It wasn't fair. It wasn't fair at all. What good was that money to the old man? But there wasn't any way to get the money.

There had been a chance, once. Long ago. That time Uncle Paul had sent him up to New York with cash and with the long list of things to buy. He had met the woman on the train. She had just acquired a Florida divorce. She was going to New York to look for work, she said.

Four days later he had awakened at noon in a third rate hotel room, with a monstrous clattering crashing hangover, soiled, wrinkled clothing, no luggage, and sixty-five cents in his pocket. The fourteen hundred dollars was gone, and the woman was gone, and there was an inch of bourbon left in a bottle. Uncle Paul had wired the money to come home on. But that was the end of it. The end of meager trust.

He remembered the black despair of that hotel room. But he had bounced back. He had forgotten it. The golden years were coming. Soon after that he had found Lenora, the girl to share the golden years. But somehow things had not worked out. Too many years had gone by. Life with the golden girl was an armed truce. He was heavy, and his head ached, and his heart pounded, and the lunch eaten hours before was an indigestible heaviness in his stomach. For the first time in his life he wondered what it would be like to die by your own hand.

CHAPTER EIGHT

Ronnie had retrieved coat, hat and suitcase, and stood on the proper corner at the proper time. There was a light at the corner, and a vacant cab stand. A gray Buick swung in toward the curb and the driver tapped the horn ring lightly, three times. Ronnie had opened the suitcase in the men's room at the station. The topcoat hung over his arm, covering his hand. He held a short-barreled Colt .38 in the concealed hand, a Detective Special. His other hand gun, a .357 Magnum, was still in the suitcase. Neither gun had ever killed. He had a proper license for both of them.

As with other guns in the past, once they had been used, he would dispose of them. No casual toss into shallow water. No quick throw into heavy brush. He would strip the gun down into its component parts. He would malform the barrel with a heavy sledge. He would bury the parts separately with as much care as though he were disposing of the body itself.

Ace opened the door and Ronnie got into the car and pulled the door shut. "Greetings," he said.

"You look sharp," said the Ace.

"I'm a tourist. A nice sharp tourist. How's Mullin?"

"Jumpy. Wouldn't you be?"

"I wouldn't know. Are you jumpy too, Ace?"

"I don't much like working with him. And I don't like working with you. But this one smells fat."

"I have no opinion about working with you. We have different specialties."

"Thank God for that. You give me the God damn creeps, kid. What are you doing in a deal like this?"

"A change of pace."

"It better be a change. Just wave the gun. Don't use it."

"I was told Mullin was running this."

"He is. But I want it to be smooth."

"Where's the pad? Out of town?"

"Not far from here. Nice place. Mullin brought a woman."

"Is that bright?"

"She's all right. Name of Sally Leon. She'll be no trouble."

"So you don't like working with me, Ace."

"No."

Ronnie shrugged and left it at that. He had long since gotten accustomed to the attitude of those who had heard rumors about him. They could understand reasons for death. Woman trouble. Or a cross. Or a quick profit. But they couldn't understand the executioner. Or feel comfortable with him.

"Is this a bank?" Ronnie asked.

"Hell no! Where have you been? Nobody messes with banks any more. It's too federal. Just punks try it. It doesn't work any more. It isn't professional."

"What is it, then?"

"Mullin can brief you. Here we are, anyhow. There isn't time to go into it."

They went into the kitchen. The woman sat at the kitchen table reading a magazine. Ronnie had slipped the revolver into his side pocket. It had been a precaution. He did not like getting into strange cars. Something could have gone sour. Somebody could have tipped the Ace. But it was still all set. So the gun could be put aside until the right time came.

The woman looked up. Ace said, "Sal, this is Ronnie."

Ronnie nodded. He liked the way she looked. He liked big blonde women. This one had no arrogance. She seemed quiet and humble and acquiescent. She acted beat down.

He knew why when Mullin came out into the kitchen. The man looked lean, mean and jumpy. He needed a shave. "Hello, kid. We've been waiting. Come on in the other room. You're due for a briefing."

They went into the big living room. Ronnie sat beside

Ace on the couch. Mullin paced back and forth and out-
lined the proposition. Ronnie listened and found himself
liking it. It sounded safe. It sounded profitable. He'd been
told to use his own judgment.

"How many in the house again?"

"The old man. A chunky colored boy about forty-five.
A punk about twenty-five or six, and his wife about
twenty-two or three."

"So why did you need me?"

"I asked for a gun. Ace is on the box. You have to
think about the car too. Two can be risky. I'm too hot
to contact local talent. I need somebody recommended. I
want to figure it all so it will go smooth. Like silk and
cream. No pain and no strain. And no shooting unless it
has to be that way. You understand that?"

"I understand it."

"What did you bring?"

"A Detective Special and a Magnum."

"I've got a Luger and six clips. Ace has got nothing.
Ace, you want the Magnum?"

"I've never carried one in my life. I'm not starting here."

"You saw the layout, Ace. Tell him."

"High stone fence around a half acre of land. Phone
lines come in over the fence from the west. Big iron gate
in the front. Usually it's closed, and probably locked.
The first-story windows on the stone house are barred.
I got a glance at the garage. Two car deal and it looks
like the jig lives over it. It is set into the northwest corner
of the area. The house is about in the middle."

"Burglar alarms?"

"Maybe. We don't know yet. We've got to make sure
of that, Harry says."

"How do we do that?"

Mullin spoke up. "The Ace has checked on the punk.
He's the only one who leaves the place. He goes to town
about every other afternoon. He sponges drinks, does a
little bowling. Ace knows him by sight. You make the
contact with him. You and Sal. Buy him drinks. Tell him
he's a great guy. You know the routine. He stayed home

today. Tomorrow, Thursday, he'll probably go into town. He drives an old tan Chev. You'll get what you can out of him. If you load him right, maybe he'll take the pair of you back to the house. That would be the best, but maybe it won't be necessary."

"Fine," Ronnie said. "I go back to the house, maybe wearing a sign that says thief?"

"Don't sweat. They won't check you too close. When we go in for the score we go in wearing masks. The Ace picked them up today at the five and dime. Ape masks. Good ones. Two bucks apiece. They'll be so busy with looking at the ape faces, they won't see anything else. Sal stays in the car. She gives us the horn if anything goes sour outside. Go get the map, Ace."

The big man brought the map back. He unfolded it and the three of them knelt on the floor. It was a decorative map of Flamingo, in color, with pictures of palm trees and orange trees.

"Here," said Mullin, "is where we are. There's the Tomlin house. If everything goes all right tomorrow, we can set it for five o'clock on Friday. There won't be any deliveries to the house after that time. It will be the best time to do it. If it goes right, we can be out of there by five-thirty. Here's the route I marked. Ace said the streets are okay. Five miles east of here we run into the Tamiami Trail. Route 41. We can follow that right up to Tampa. We'll try to get a motel as near the city as we can. There's a lot of vacancies right now. Sticking to the speed limit, it should take us about an hour and a half to get to Tampa. We make the split right there, and we split up right there. You can leave by train or plane or whatever you think you want to do."

"It sounds all right," Ronnie said. "If it's one-tenth the money you think is in there, it still sounds all right."

"It better be more than a tenth. I need more than a tenth. Here's the routine when we go in. We round up the four of them. You keep a gun on them while the Ace takes a look at the box. He has some stuff to work with. If it looks too rough, we'll have to persuade the old guy. Roughing up the girl will probably do it. Once we get it open, we have to keep them quiet. Tomorrow try to find out if there's any place in the house where we can lock them up. We could use an hour. Ace will have the plates dirtied up. I'm going to have to ditch the car, so watch prints. And watch prints in the house here, too. Once the time is set, we'll give the house a good cleaning."

They talked some more. Ace brought in three cans of beer. Ronnie sat in a deep chair and sipped the beer. He reminded himself to wipe the beer can clean before throwing it out. It wouldn't make much difference if the others forgot that little detail.

He sat in the deep chair and listened to them talk and plan. He looked at the Ace's thick neck, and the bald spot that gleamed in the lights. The plan sounded all right. Now it was time to begin to integrate his own plan with theirs. Ace was the primary assignment. But nothing could be done about the Ace until after the box was open. The old man might drop dead of a heart attack and be unable to give the combination.

It might work right there in the stone house. Ace and Mullin, quickly, after the box was open. But the girl would be outside, in the car, and that was a complication. Not in the stone house. Get the money into the car. Get rolling. But once the money was in the car, both Mullin and the Ace would be more on guard. That was the time when accidents happened too often, between the take and the cut. Mullin might even be planning a little accident for the two of them. He had nothing to lose. Any fracas as they were getting into the car would cut down on the getaway time.

It had to happen in the stone house, or before they set out for the stone house. If it happened in the stone house, it might make sense to take the whole lot of them, the whole seven, the five men and the two women. He might get the blonde in the house on some pretext. Then close the big gates and drive away. Load the car and drive away.

The thought of taking the whole seven of them made

him feel excited. It made his hands wet. It was good to think about, but it didn't make sense. It would make the whole thing too heavy. The whole damn country would be hunting for him.

Then he knew what he would have to do. He would have to take a chance on their not needing the Ace. Once the time was set, Mullin would want to go through with it, even if there was just the two of them. Mullin would have to go through with it. There wasn't anything else he could do. And no one else he could get to help him.

Ronnie became intensely aware of the Ace. It was always that way. A heightening of curiosity. He could see the Ace more vividly. To Ronnie, the Ace had a death-marked look. How many more beats in that heavy heart? How many more gestures of the thick hands? Ronnie felt the god-power in himself. The power to glaze those eyes and still the breath and turn the man into nothing. Into damp clay.

"You following this?" Mullin asked him sharply.

"I've got it all straight."

The woman in the kitchen could hear their low voices. She sat at the table looking down at the magazine, but she did not see the words on the cheap paper. She was thinking of the strange road she had traveled, the road that had brought Sally Leon at last to this particular Wednesday night, to this Florida town, to this time of waiting and listening to the men in the other room.

She wondered what Barney Shuseck would think of her now if he could see her. She wondered if he would feel anger, or contempt. It had always been difficult to guess what Barney would think, to guess what Barney would do. Maybe that had been part of the attraction.

In the beginning was the Dream. The Dream of a small solemn blonde girl, fifth daughter of a factory worker in Dearborn. She was no good in school. The Dream was the only important thing. It always had the same ending —the black limousine pulling up to the marquee, the police holding the crowd back, searchlight beams cutting across the dark blue velvet of the California sky. "Hey, it's Sally Leon!" they would yell and the police would strain to hold them back.

It's Sally Leon! Regal in sables, smiling brilliantly and nodding to her fans, walking between the packed throngs into the movie, sitting there with people who adored her, to watch the first showing of the film that would win the Oscar.

She was poor in her schoolwork. She had little interest in boys. Her only interest in money was to have enough to go to every movie that showed in the area and buy every fan magazine that came out. She spent hours before her mirror. She imitated the stars. Her family was amused and exasperated by her. So intense was her dream world that she found it difficult to follow the simplest household directions. In that house there was neither time nor energy to concentrate on the emotional problems of one daughter—particularly one who made no trouble, who moved dimly through life, engrossed in the Dream.

When she was fifteen she left and went to Hollywood. She registered with Central Casting. She was fired from two car hop jobs because she could not remember orders. She attended premieres, crowding close as she could get, staring wide-eyed at the stars, perfectly confident that she would be one some day. She was fired from a department store job in Los Angeles. The supervisor for the floor told her she was too absent-minded. She kept the next job, as waitress in a tavern, for quite a long time.

The first man came along when she was seventeen. He knew the language of the studios. He said he was an assistant producer. He said he could get her a screen test. He lived in one of a string of attached bungalows which encircled a court with a small fountain that didn't work. She moved in with him. He made it quite clear that this was the way you got into the movies. He stalled on the screen test for nearly two months, and then a woman in one of the other bungalows told her the man was a studio electrician. She was not hurt or angry. She was impatient at the delay. She moved out, got her job back, and began haunting Central Casting again.

The next man was more plausible. He said he was an agent, and in a sense he was, though he kept his office in his jacket pocket. He got her three days' work. It was a college picture. She had to sit in the stands with a lot of other girls and smile and yell and wave a banner. She received twenty dollars a day. When the picture came out five months later she found that she was not in it. That scene had been cut. She sat through three showings and made absolutely certain that she was not in it. It was disappointing as she had sent a card to her family telling them she was in the picture. She was ashamed of that, and so she never contacted them again in any way. It was the third and last postcard she ever sent them.

She lived with Wally for seven months. He had a violent temper. He could not seem to get her into any other pictures. In the beginning he financed voice lessons for her, but later he did not want to continue the expense. When he got tired of her, he passed her along to a younger friend, a man who was trying to write scripts. When the younger man left to go to New York, she kept the room they had lived in and got a job as a waitress and kept trying to get into the movies. She had learned to carry herself a little better, and modulate her speaking voice, and sing in a small clear alto. She tried dancing lessons, but found she had no aptitude. It was hard for her to move quickly enough.

A girl she worked with told her she had enough looks so that maybe she could get a job in a club, and told her how to go about it. She went to the club in the early afternoon. It was the afternoon of her nineteenth birthday. After he had talked to her for about five minutes, the man locked the door of his small office. She accepted him without struggle, the way she had learned to accept. It had seemed important with the first man, but now it no longer seemed important. It was a mechanical thing. Sometimes it was pleasurable, and sometimes it was not. It was a means to an end, and thus must be endured.

This was one of the more unpleasant times, but that evening she became a part of the show, a part of the finale. She wore a soiled girdle of feathers around her hips. Her breasts were bare. She had to stand absolutely still, bathed in a strange green light, while a girl whose costume was fresher and whose breasts were covered did a contortionist act. Three other girls stood as Sally stood while the act went on. Sally was pleased to note that they were all older than she was, and not nearly as pretty.

It was a man who came to the Blue Onyx Club who finally got her into the movies. He was a thin bald nervous man with a loose mouth and a deep Pacific tan. He took her at three in the morning, after the last show, to a barren rundown building in a shabby part of Los Angeles. Two other cars were parked behind the building. The man parked his convertible beside them and they went into the building. There was a cameraman, an electrician, another man of the same breed as the man who brought her, and a muscular young man with a dull sleepy expression.

There were no introductions. The cameraman looked at Sally carefully. "This is better stuff than those last pigs. You sure you want to do this, kid?"

Then she was told what she would have to do. She did not want to do it. But they all acted so matter-of-fact about it. And Mr. Binder, the man who brought her, told her the makeup would be pretty heavy, and she could fix her hair a little different. She was still reluctant and Mr. Binder said he would make it a hundred and a half instead of a hundred. She had never done anything like it before. She was scared and awkward. Finally they felt they had enough, and the sun was out when Binder drove her home.

She made seven pictures. The instructions were easy to follow. The pictures were nearly all the same. Binder finally let her see one. She paid no attention to what she was doing in the short sound picture. She was only interested in how she looked, how her voice sounded, how she walked and held herself. She knew at once that she was looking at a stranger, not at the creature in the Dream. She looked at a girl with a ripe heavy body and a blank face and a thin squeaky voice and dull eyes. The Dream died there.

Binder came to the Blue Onyx once more.

"We got to fold for a while, kid. They staked the place out and they were ready to pick us up, but we got a tip. We'll be back in business in a couple of months. I'll look you up."

"I guess I don't want to do that any more."

Binder gave her a weary look. "You might as well. I was in legitimate movies for eighteen years. I know the score, kid. For this kind of stuff, you've got it. You've got all you need. For the legitimate stuff, you haven't got it. You don't project. You move around like a zombie. You're built real good, though, and that's just about all we need. So you might as well stick with this. The money doesn't hurt you any, does it?"

"I guess I don't want to do it any more."

"There's plenty who will," he said.

She wanted to get away from the Dream. She went to Chicago. By then she had contacts, and she got a job doing a slow strip in a cellar club. She lived with the horn player in the band. She felt half dead. Once in a while they'd let her do a vocal. She added bumps and grinds to her thin voice and put the songs over after a fashion. She met Barney Shuseck in that cellar club. He was different. By then there had been a lot of men. Violent men, petty men, discouraged men, selfish men. Barney was not like the others. She could talk to Barney. He listened to her. He understood her.

"Sure, I get it. You couldn't make it—so you couldn't make it. We'll have us a movie, kid. I'm a killer and a thief and a two-time loser, and you're my girl. Like in the movies. See?"

And that is what he was. A thief and a killer and a two-time loser. She was with him for three years, until she was twenty-four. His money bought expensive clothes. They lived well. They saw a lot of the country. He could be unexpectedly tender, and unexpectedly brutal. He broke her arm and bought her an emerald on the same day. He bought the emerald from a fence.

He was working with Danny Riverio—not with him but for him—when he was shot and killed by a rookie patrolman. Riverio felt a certain degree of responsibility for her after she endured a full week of questioning without telling the authorities anything. He put her in the club of a friend of his in Detroit. He saw that she was set up in a fairly good apartment. Once in a while he would send friends to her to be entertained. Then he had sent her up to the lake to entertain Harry Mullin. Mullin wanted to keep her for a while. Riverio didn't care. So she had come along. She could have avoided coming along, but it didn't seem to make much difference one way or the other.

Mullin was a type with which she was familiar. Silent, sour, nervous, domineering. There was no tenderness in him. She accepted him, as she had accepted the others. Once the Dream died, it didn't make much difference. Now Mullin, the Ace and Ronnie were on a job. She knew she would be frightened while it was going on. She knew she would be glad when it was over. She had no idea what would become of her when it was over. She would go out of the country with Harry, if they made a big score. That might be nice. She had never been out of the country. She wondered what it was like.

Ronnie pushed the swinging door open and came out into the kitchen. She glanced at him and then looked back at the magazine. She heard him go behind her and get a can of beer out of the refrigerator. She heard the hiss as he punched holes in the top of the can.

She stiffened as he put his fingers on the nape of her neck under her hair and caressed her.

"You shouldn't ought to do that," she said.

He didn't stop. "I do lots of things I shouldn't ought to."

"It will make trouble."

"Everybody's got trouble."

"Don't. Please."

He laughed softly and then he stopped. He said, "Aren't you maybe too much woman for that burned-out Mullin?"

She didn't answer and he was moving toward the door when Mullin came out into the kitchen, his mouth ugly. "How long does it take you to get yourself a beer, kid?"

"I was talking to Sal here," Ronnie said easily.

"Don't talk to her."

Ronnie shrugged. "Suit yourself." He walked on into the other room and the door swung shut.

"He make a pass?"

"No, Harry. No pass, honest."

"Tell me if he does. And if Ace does either."

"I'll tell you, Harry."

"Make some sandwiches."

She got up quickly and went to the breadbox. She imagined she could still feel the touch of Ronnie's fingers on the nape of her neck. It gave her an odd feeling. He was a strange man. He wasn't like all the others. There was something very different about him. Almost creepy. Maybe it was something about his eyes.

CHAPTER NINE

When Ben Piersall arrived at his downtown office in the Flamingo Bank and Trust Company Building at eight-thirty on Thursday morning, he noticed Dr. Tomlin's shiny old black Packard in a parking place near the bank, with Arnold Addams in his chauffeur hat standing near it.

He thought little of it and was astonished when he found Dr. Tomlin seated in the small ante-room. Lorraine Bibbs, Ben's middle-aged secretary, gave him a nervous smile and greeting. She was one of the local people thoroughly terrified of the austere Dr. Tomlin.

Dr. Tomlin got up as Ben came in. They greeted each other and Dr. Tomlin said, "Please forgive me for not making an appointment, Ben."

"It isn't necessary for you to do that at any time."

"I like to use common courtesy. This won't take very long. I used to impose on your father, too."

"I don't think he ever minded, either. Come on in, Doctor."

They went into his private office and Ben closed the door. Dr. Tomlin seated himself across the desk, took a document from an inside pocket and handed it to Ben. "I guess you've never seen this. It's my will. Your father drew it up. I asked him not to keep a copy here. Mind reading it over?"

"Not at all." It did not take long to scan the will. It was not complicated. It established a trust fund for Dillon and Lenora Parks and it left them the house. After taxes were paid, and after a cash bequest to Arnold Addams, the remainder of the estate was to be divided equally among the medical research foundations listed.

"I assume you wish to change it."

"I want to include Laurie Preston, Mrs. Joseph Preston. I want a trust fund to be set up for her to take effect upon my death. It should provide a life income of five hundred dollars a month. She's the girl who is staying with me. Laurie and her husband. They're remote relatives."

"That can be done easily."

"And I'd like to increase the cash bequest to Arnold."

"In that case, Doctor, rather than adding a codicil, I think we should rewrite the whole document."

"Can it be done quickly?"

"I can have it ready today, if you wish."

"I would appreciate it, Ben. I . . . I don't expect to die today or tomorrow or next week. As a doctor, I know I'm in better shape than I deserve. But I've had a feeling of impending catastrophe. Like some superstitious old lady. I'll feel better when the new document is signed and legal."

Ben had been observing the old man carefully. There was the inescapable feebleness of age, but the eyes, and the brain behind them, seemed as sharp as ever.

"Can I speak frankly, Doctor Tomlin?"

"Your father always did. Certainly."

"You are an old man. A lot of the people around here consider you to be a very eccentric old man. Just to be perfectly safe about this, I'd like to make two appointments for you. I'd like to have you go to two doctors today and have them examine you and have them make a written report on you. On your sanity."

Tomlin's face darkened and his voice grew thick. "Absolute nonsense!" he shouted.

"Now wait a minute. You want this will to stand up."

"Of course!"

"If anybody should want to try to break it after your death they would try to prove that you were mentally incompetent at the time you revised your will."

Dr. Tomlin relaxed visibly. "That would be typical of the reasoning of my grandniece, Lenora."

"I'm not naming any names. I'd feel better if those two dated medical reports were on file with the original of the will. I think you will feel better also, Doctor."

Tomlin smiled faintly and said, "I'm sorry. For a moment my attitude wasn't exactly professional. I'll do what you suggest, of course."

Ben Piersall shifted his desk chair uneasily. "There's something else I want to ask you about, Doctor. Please understand that I'm bringing this up because I'm trying to protect your interests."

"I understand that."

"Last evening I had a phone call from Bud Hedges. You know him pretty well."

"I know Benjamin. He's a bit of an old lady. He has a shrewd eye for land values. If you want to pick up a piece of land quietly, he isn't the man to use. He talks too much."

"He called me last night, Doctor. At first I didn't know what was on his mind. Then he brought the conversation around to the phone conversation he had with you yesterday afternoon."

"I haven't seen or spoken to Benjamin in months."

"What!"

"That's quite correct. I've had no contact with him whatsoever."

"That's very strange. I thought Hedges had misunderstood what you wanted him to do. He claims you called him and asked him to get prices on a lot of land on Flamingo Key. He said you spoke as though you didn't know the causeway had been put in. He said you talked as though it was twenty-five years ago, when the key had some fishing shacks on it and nothing much else. I thought it was strange."

Dr. Tomlin looked at him oddly. "But not too strange?"

Ben flushed. "Hedges is a gossip, but he isn't a liar. I'll be honest with you. I thought the call *could* have occurred."

"And you thought I could be losing touch with reality. What do you think now?"

"I don't know what to think, Doctor."

Tomlin leaned back. "It puts me in an odd position. I don't know what to think either. Professionally I could understand it. I know what age does. I've seen the effect of delusion, loss of memory. Benjamin would recognize my voice."

"But you have no recollection of making any such call."

"I am morally certain that I didn't. I've been reviewing what I did yesterday. I can account for all my time. What time did I call him? Can you find out?"

Ben phoned Hedges' office. Hedges was in. "This is Ben Piersall. Say, what time did Doctor Tomlin phone you yesterday?"

"Hold it a minute. I've got it right here on my pad. I mark down the time calls come in. Sometimes it's important. Here it is. Twenty-five minutes of four. Why?"

"Thanks a lot, Bud. I appreciate it." He hung up and said, "Twenty-five minutes of four, Doctor."

"I took a nap in the afternoon. At about four-fifteen I went for a short drive with Laurie. Arnold drove the car. We drove south. We didn't stop. We returned to the house at five. I was not near a phone during that time. Both Laurie and Arnold can confirm that. Where does that leave us?"

Ben Piersall was silent for several moments. He could hear the traffic sounds on Bay Avenue, hear the clack of Lorraine's typewriter in the outer office. "Doctor, I don't know how ethical this is, but I'm going to tell you something."

"If you can tell me anything that will make sense of this . . ."

"I ran into Lenora the other day. This may hurt. She wanted me to undertake something. She wanted me to help her try to get you committed to an institution as mentally incompetent."

He watched Dr. Tomlin closely. The old man seemed to shrink in upon himself, to grow older within the space of a few seconds. His eyes looked vague and puzzled. His voice was weaker. "You know all along that they are greedy people. And they are selfish people. You recognize that, but you think there is some warmth there—some pride—some decency. It just seems . . ."

"I told her she was a fool. Apparently it was more her idea than Dil's."

"She is an unscrupulous girl."

"I'm afraid so. This may be a wild guess, Doctor, but it would explain the phone call. Somebody pretending to be you. Lennie could have instigated it. You see how it would work. This call to Hedges. He'll tell dozens of people. There'd be other calls. There probably will be. Then, with half the town talking about you, she might get some lawyer who would handle it, and there might be enough evidence to make it stick. This could be very bad, Doctor."

"What can we do?"

"Get the will fixed up as quickly as possible. And then—"

"Wait a moment. She came to the house. She had a man with her, a man named Mooney. He apparently works for Dil. I couldn't understand why she came to see me. Her excuse was worthless. That man could be helping her."

"It's possible."

"Could you find out?"

"I don't know. Possibly. It would be a difficult thing to check on."

"I want you to check on it. In the meantime we will go ahead with the will, with one change. I do not wish to seem vindictive. Eliminate the trust fund for Dillon and Lenora. Change it to a cash bequest of . . . five hundred dollars. Leave the house to Laurie Preston. Do that first, Ben, and then investigate Lenora. If your guess is wrong, there will be time enough to make out another will, reinstating the trust fund and leaving them the house. I hope your guess is wrong. I can forgive her being so greedy as to try to have me put away. But I could not forgive her for . . . compounding my eccentricities."

Strength and force had come back to the old man. Ben said, "I'll do that, Doctor. I'm glad you came in."

"I'm grateful to you for being frank with me."

"Doctor, we could do this less dramatically. We could make out the new will the way you originally instructed me. Then I could tell Lenora the terms of the will and the precautions we have taken to keep it from being broken. I note here that the bank is the executor. She's shrewd enough to recognize a stalemate. If she's behind the Hedges phone call, she'd stop that nonsense immediately."

"I think I prefer that it be done this way, Ben."

"Then let's get to work. I'll make the appointments for you right now. The will can be ready for signatures by three this afternoon."

At one o'clock on Thursday afternoon Ronnie sat behind the wheel of the gray Buick. Sally Leon sat beside him. They were parked two blocks from the Tomlin home, on the route to the downtown section. The angular patterns of the shade of palm fronds partially shielded the car from the high hot sun, but enough sun touched the metal to make the inside of the car uncomfortably hot. They had all the car windows rolled down. Their faces were damp with sweat. Ronnie's white shirt stuck to his back. The girl sat completely relaxed, her skirt hiked well above her knees, heavy thighs spread, her hair damp at her temples.

"So we sit here all afternoon," Ronnie said with muted savagery.

"It's pretty hot."

"It's pretty hot. It's pretty hot. It can cook you. Jesus, you have a lot of sparkling conversation."

"What do you want to talk about?"

"You, my darling. Your incredible beauty. Your elfin charm. Your gay little mannerisms."

"You talk funny."

"What's your vocabulary, sweets? Eight hundred words? You could use sign language and grunt once in a while and get along just fine. I would find you delightful in bed, but lambie, you are pretty sodden in the discussion department."

"Harry said for you not to make any passes."

"I must correct your grammar. Harry said for me not to make *no* passes."

She stirred and said sullenly, "You're so damn smart."

"That's the tricky part. I am smart. They proved it to me. They gave me tests. They said, Ronald, you have a superior mind. We wish to help you, Ronald. We wish to make a good citizen out of you, Ronald. You can become a good citizen and have a wife and kiddies and spend all day in an office, and owe on the car and owe on the TV, and owe on the mortgage, and buy a lot of nice insurance so that when the ulcer gets you, or the heart or something, the kiddies can keep going to school and eventually your loving wife can go sit on her fat ass in the sun and improve hell out of her canasta."

"I'd like to have kids."

"Why don't you? Sows should be surrounded by the scampering piglets and watch them turn into shoats."

"You don't have to be so damn nasty."

"Ronald, they told me. We have given up. We cannot turn you into a good citizen, Ronald, because you refuse to cooperate. Something was left out of you, Ronald, when you were assembled. One dedicated young one called me a psychopath. One emotional old one told me I had no soul."

"You talk an awful lot."

"Darleeng, tonight we shall slip an Oriental drug into Harry's cambric tea. Then you come tippy-toe to my boudoir and we shall make the illicit luff."

"You shouldn't ought to talk like that."

He turned in the seat and took hold of her arm above the elbow. "Now we talk serious-like, angel."

"You're hurting me."

"What if something happened to the Ace, and something else happened to Mullin?"

"What do you mean?"

"These things can go sour. I come running out of the house. Ace and Mullin lie in there in a welter of blood. I come panting out, carrying a fortune in cash. What then, angel?"

"You mean if just you and me are left?"

"Splendid! You're catching on."

"I guess we would have to leave and go some place else."

"It wouldn't be wise to sit there in front of the house then, would it?"

"No, but . . ."

"Then what will life hold for us, darleeng? You and me and incredible riches. Two young things fleeing together, brought closer by tension and danger. Clinging to each other with tearful kissings."

"You mix me all up."

"Okay den, babe. I give it to youse straight, see. You're wit dis Mullin, see. So he's dead, see. Den you and me, we hit the road togedder, hey?"

She scowled at him. "You're all the time making fun of me. I don't like it."

"I'm sorry. May I have your decision?"

"If you go out of the country, I'd like to come along. I want to go to a foreign country. I've never been."

"This is the beginning of a deathless romance." He looked in the rear vision mirror. "And here comes our target for today, I think."

The ancient tan Chevy rattled by them down the quiet palm-lined street. Ronnie caught a glimpse of the man behind the wheel. He fitted the description. He started the Buick and put it in gear. "And away we go," he said softly.

They saw Joe Preston leave the tan car in the sun outside the bowling alley and amble in. Ronald Crown swung in and parked beside the old tan car. He took the key from the ignition and turned to the girl.

"Give this character the business, Sal. He doesn't look bright. He's got to think you're the most available item that's come along in years. He's got to think you've fallen for him. You and I are just friends. We met down here. I'm going to be dumb, friendly and generous. Can you bowl?"

"I used to go with a fellow that liked to. He taught me."

"Okay. I don't bowl. Just follow the leads, angel."

It was a white stucco building with a Nissen roof, with glass brick on either side of the entrance. An unlighted red neon sign stretched across the pasty front of the building, saying in big letters, *Bowlarama*. As Ronnie pushed the door open he heard the drone of a ball on maple, the splashing clatter of pinfall, the chunk and clank of automatic pinsetters. There were a dozen alleys, four of them brightly lighted and in use. There was a smell of beer and chalk and perspiration.

He paused in the dimness, the girl beside him, and saw Joe Preston renting a pair of shoes. He nudged the girl and they moved over to the window. Preston turned away from the window. As he heard Sally asking for bowling shoes, Ronnie caught up with Preston and said, "You all alone?"

"Why?" Preston asked, dimly belligerent.

"My friend there, getting her shoes, doesn't like to bowl alone. I got a sore back. You want to bowl with her, I can keep score for you."

He saw Joe Preston turn and look at Sally. Preston had a lean pallid face, long sideburns, hollows in his cheeks, hair worn long and brushed back at the temples. He wore his cigarette with Bogart mannerisms. His features, separately, seemed good enough. But the total effect was one of dimness, vagueness, lack of identity. Ronnie guessed that Joe Preston thought of himself as handsome and tough. But the facade looked brittle. One casual backhand from a cop would create the sniveler. Ronnie had seen a lot of them. They dwelt on the fringe of evil. He had never had to kill one. They never became that important. He saw the face tighten with pleasure and anticipation.

"Sure. I'll bowl with her."

"Thanks a lot. I don't know how good she is. Just met her the other day. Maybe she'll slow up your game."

"I'm not too sharp at it."

The girl came up to them. "This is Sally. I'm Ronnie."

"My name is Joe." They all shook hands. Sally pulled herself close to Joe during the handshake, holding it overlong, looking into his eyes. Ronnie watched Joe react, coloring a bit, licking his lip, looking sidelong at Ronnie.

The manager lighted alley six for them. Ronnie bought beers at the counter and brought them over. Sally had selected a ball. She wore a pale yellow sleeveless blouse, a skirt of very pale aqua which was tight across her hips, pleated and flaring at the hem. Bowling is a harsh test for a woman. She can look grotesque and ludicrous—a clown spectacle of ungainly hips and awkward knees— or she can make of the act of running to the foul line and releasing the ball a rhythmic and enticing thing, unaccountably sexual, peculiarly exciting. Ronnie watched Sally move forward and release the ball. She moved slowly, and with humid deep-loined grace—a ripe Diana hunting slowly, flexing, waiting, rising, turning, walking back with faint sated smile.

The next time she bowled he watched Joe Preston's expression. A hungry bass would wear that expression in the instant before the heavy lips find the concealed sharpness of the hook.

When Joe bowled, it was with an awareness of the girl watching him. He bowled with great dash. He hurled the ball with great force and speed. He jumped high in the air when the ball hooked into the pocket and the pins exploded, turning with flushed proud grinning face, a dank lock of hair across the pale forehead, taking a small red comb from his pocket to put the hair back in gleaming place as he returned to watch Ronnie mark the strike. Joe was a boy hanging from his heels from a high limb. Or a horseman, dipping his lance on parade as he passed the stands.

They bowled. Ronnie bought beer and kept score and paid for the games. He knew that Joe Preston had become almost unaware of his presence. Sally gave all her attention to Joe. Her face glowed and she laughed out loud several times. Ronnie realized that it was not all an act, that the girl was really having fun. It was the type of

108 • John D. MacDonald

irony that Ronnie appreciated. Here, for a little time, she was completely at home.

After three games Sally inspected her thumb and said, "Gee, that better be the last one. I'm getting a blister."

"Let me see," Joe said. They stood close together looking down at the sore thumb, their heads almost touching. "I guess you better quit at that, Sally."

"Let's go find a nice dark bar," Ronnie said. "The three of us. Unless you want to hang around here."

"No. I've had enough. I think that would be fine."

"Finish your beer and we'll take off."

They went out into the glare of the sunlight. The three of them went in the Buick. Joe gave directions. The bar was narrow and dark and air-conditioned, dwarfed by a juke box that exceeded the dreams of Persian kings. They took a back booth, Joe and Sally on one side, Ronnie facing them. A bored bartender in a dirty apron came back to take the order.

"I'm going to switch from beer, people," Ronnie said. "Double bourbon on the rocks. This is on me. How about three of those?"

"Sure," Sally said. "Beer bloats me up."

Joe made a token protest about paying, and ordered the same. When the bartender set the drinks down, the one he set in front of Ronnie slopped over. The man started away and Ronnie called him back.

"What do you want?"

"Go get a rag and come mop this up," Ronnie said, smiling.

"Use one of them paper napkins, doc."

Ronnie slid quickly out of the booth. He was still smiling. His voice was very soft. "I don't want to get irritable. I don't want to get upset. Do you want me to get upset?"

"Well, I . . ."

"We want it nice and quiet in here. Like a mouse. We don't want any trouble. So go get your little rag and waddle back down here and wipe up what you spilled."

The man looked hesitant. He tried to smile. He said, too loudly, "Okay. Sure thing, doc."

"Sure thing, *sir*."

"Look . . ."

"Sir!"

"Yes sir." He said it as though his mouth hurt.

"And bring back the bottle and a bowl of ice."

"We don't . . ."

"Starting now, you do." Ronnie sat down leaving the man enough room to get by. He breathed deeply and easily and felt the tension within him crumble away into softness again.

"I thought you were going to have trouble there," Joe said with evident admiration.

"Not from him," Ronnie said. "Not from a tired fat man in a third-rate saloon. They can't read your cards. They look at the smile and they listen to the soft voice and they feel uncomfortable because you're standing too close. So they break it off because it's something they don't understand."

The man brought the ice and bottle. He swabbed the table top. He left without a word.

Joe turned to Sally beside him. They were sitting close. "Been down here long?"

"Not long."

"Where are you staying?"

"With friends."

"Have you been down here long, Joe?" Ronnie asked.

"A few months. The wife and I come down and moved in with a rich relative. An old duck with a big stone house. We came here from California. Los Angeles."

"Hey, I lived out there for a long time!" Sally said. Ronnie sat patiently for the fifteen minutes it took them to talk about the town and places they knew. He kept Joe's glass full. Joe drank steadily and automatically.

Joe finally turned to him and said, "You on a vacation, Ronnie?"

"I guess you could call it that. Things got a little warm. I decided it was time to leave town for a while."

Joe's eyes brightened. "Law trouble?"

"In a way."

"You know, Ronnie, I knew right off you were an operator. You know a funny thing? I got the roust out in L.A. It got to be time to leave. You know how it goes?"

"I know how it goes."

"But it was a break, me being related to the old duck."

Ronnie sneered in a delicate way. "Sure. A rich relative. Like in the fairy stories. I've heard that crap before, Joe. That car of yours. Is that your rich relative's limousine?"

Joe flushed angrily. "Take it easy. I was leveling. That's the car we come out here in. The old guy, Doctor Tomlin his name is, is loaded. Laurie, that's my wife, kind of a funny-acting kid, she gets along good with the old boy. He's paying her to stay with him. I never had it so good. No kidding. It's a big stone house and he's really loaded."

"Sure."

"Don't you believe me? Damn it, you can ask anybody in town. The people that live here. They know about him. He's got a safe in his house. He keeps it all there in cash. Maybe a million bucks. How do you like that?"

"Roll up your sleeve. I want to see where you get those dreams, Joe." He got up from the booth. "I'll be back in a few minutes, kids. I've got to make a couple of phone calls."

He went out onto the sidewalk and walked slowly to the corner. He bought cigarettes, lighted one and smoked for a time and walked slowly back. When he slid into the booth Joe had a shamefaced look. Sally's lipstick was smeared, her hair tousled.

"Honest, Ronnie, the old man . . ."

"I know, Joe. He keeps a box full of thousand-dollar bills under his bed. Have a drink."

"I guess it sounds funny, all right. Hell, what difference does it make? I'm living without working."

After a long delay, the liquor began to take effect on Joe Preston. He didn't bother to comb the dank lock back. His eyes didn't track and focus properly. His mouth was loose. He had crowded Sally back into a corner of the booth. Other customers began to arrive. Joe, thick-tongued and rambling, told Ronnie and Sally how important he had been out in Los Angeles. He dropped a few names. Ronnie knew the names, and in two cases, knew the men. He didn't let Joe know that.

Ronnie gauged the time carefully. He said, "We have to run along."

"Party's just getting under way, isn't it, honey?" Joe said to Sally. "You just run along then, Ronnie."

Sally looked at Ronnie and he shook his head. "I have to go too."

"What do you wanna do that for, honey? You know I like you? You're a dish, honey. A big beautiful dish. Like a dish of vanilla ice cream. I love ice cream."

"Maybe you can show us that big beautiful stone house you dreamed up, Joe." Ronnie said it carefully, watchfully.

Joe straightened up. "Okay, wise guy. I'll show you the house. I'll show you the whole deal, wise guy." He was full of drunken indignation.

They got him out into the Buick. He staggered badly. His face was beaded with sweat, full of a greenish pallor. Ronnie thought he had let it go too far, but Joe pulled himself back together. They stopped at the bowling alley. Joe insisted he could drive his own car. He wanted Sally to ride with him. Ronnie followed the tan Chevy. It wandered loosely down the street, nudging the curbs when it turned corners. When they came to the stone house, Joe bumped the gates with the front bumper of his car, and leaned on the horn. Ronnie saw a stocky colored man hurry out to the gates. Joe had to back off so they could be swung open. He drove through and Ronnie followed him in the Buick.

Joe stumbled out of the car and made a wide sweep of his arm toward the house and said, "Told you! Great big stone son of a bitch, isn't it?"

Sally had gotten out on the other side. Joe tried to go around his own car, but blundered into the fender and bounced off to land on his hands and knees. Sally helped him up and he clung to her, his arm around her neck, smiling foolishly at the sturdy young woman with sun-streaked hair who came around the corner of the house.

"Hey Laurie. Wancha meet some friends of mine. Laurie, this is Sally. And he's Ronnie. Nice people."

Sally was trying to disentangle herself from Joe's heavy arm. Laurie looked irritated and angered. She acknowledged the introductions with a cold nod. Ronnie moved closer to her and said in a low tone, "I thought we'd better see that he got home okay."

"He doesn't look very okay."

"He'll fold up in a few minutes. How about my helping you get him to bed?"

"We can manage, thank you."

Ronnie went over and pulled Joe free of Sally. "Come on, fella. You're going to bed."

"Nuts. It's early. It's daylight. See that house. Got half the money in the world in there. Honest. The doc is a stingy old son of a . . ."

"Joe!" Laurie said sharply.

He grinned at her. "Sorry, button. I just . . ." The grin faded and his color went bad. He turned toward the nearby hedge. Ronnie went with him and held him and kept him from falling as he vomited. "Guess I better . . . go to bed," Joe mumbled.

"Lead the way," Ronnie said to Laurie.

"There's no need to . . ."

"It's no trouble. If I let go now, he'll drop." Joe stood limply erect, sagging against Ronnie, his eyes half closed.

Laurie shrugged and turned. Ronnie followed her in, urging Joe along. An old man stood in the lower hallway.

"What is this?" he demanded.

"Joe got drunk and some people brought him home, Doctor Paul." She did not attempt to make any introductions. The staircase was wide. Wide enough so that Laurie took Joe's other arm and helped with him. Joe was mumbling but Ronnie could not understand what he said. They went down a long wide hallway to a room near the back of the house. He held Joe while she took the spread off the big double bed. She turned the crisp white sheet back. Ronnie turned Joe around and let him down. Joe sat on the edge of the bed, elbows on his knees, head lowered. Laurie pushed him gently back. Ronnie saw the unexpected tenderness in her face. She was, Ronnie decided, a farm type. Milk maid. Hay mows and barn dances—and a good thing to have in a feather bed when the winter nights were long and cold.

She knelt to take off his shoes. As she worked at the laces she looked obliquely up at Ronnie, tossing her head to get the streaky hair away from her eye. "Really, I can manage now. Thank you."

"I can find my way out."

She stood up. "I'm sorry. I'll come down . . ."

"Stay with your boy. Get him tucked in. It's okay. Glad to help out."

"I'm sorry I was cross. But seeing him come home like that. It hasn't happened in a long time."

"Not since Los Angeles?"

She looked at him steadily. "That's right. Not since Los Angeles."

He went down the stairs alone. The lower hallway was empty. He went over to an open doorway and looked into the study. The walls were lined with books. The old man was reading a newspaper. He looked up at Ronnie.

"Well, we got him in okay."

"Splendid," the old man said absently and raised the newspaper again.

"I'm surprised a punk like that lives in a layout like this."

The old man lowered the paper and stared at him. "Are you? It is surprising, isn't it? Good day."

"Goodbye."

Sally was standing by the Buick. The Negro stood by the open gates. Ronnie motioned Sally into the car, got in behind the wheel and backed violently out.

"You know," Sally said, "he's a real nice fellow."

"He's just dandy. A bowling fool."

"It was nice to bowl again. I could do better the next time, maybe."

"For Christ sake, shut up!"

She flounced further away from him and they did not speak again on the way back to the rented house on Huntington Drive.

CHAPTER TEN

Lenora Parks had spent two hours of Thursday morning on the private gulf beach in front of their Seascape Estates home, coming in only when it was time to pay off the woman who had spent the morning cleaning the house. She had spent part of the two hours with a neighbor and had been glad when the neighbor had gone home to change and go marketing. She liked the solitude of the beach, liked the wave sound and the feel of the sun on her body. She liked to roll over on the fleecy blanket and press her body against the sun-hot sand underneath. Solitude was always good. But today there was more reason than before to be alone and to think.

She knew that she could not use her mind the way she would like to use it. It would be good to be able to pile thoughts and plans and conclusions one on the other like blocks, keeping the edges squared and making a sturdy structure. But her thoughts seemed more like little silver darts that flashed across consciousness, embedding themselves in random targets. She could not close out the world and think. The world presented myriad sensual stimuli and these deflected the silver darts. Out on the beach the sun heat had softened her thoughts into a drugged and lazy optimism. Everything was going to work out. The good years were ahead.

But now she was back in the house, in the shower stall, soaping her breasts while the needle spray stung her back, and it did not look as though anything was going to work out for her, ever. Thirty-five years had gone by, and nothing was the way she had planned it. Nothing was as she thought it would be. Things had gone off the track when she had lost Ben Piersall, long ago. Ben was now an adult, a man of warmth and strength and certainty.

And she was married to a child. A balding, heavy-bellied, querulous, disappointing child.

She had no illusions about his faithfulness. There had been affairs for her throughout the years of marriage. Far too many of them. She had sought a little gleam of magic. All she had received was the excitement of stolen pleasure, the mild contempt of the community, a certain adeptness in the arts of physical love, a practiced caution and slyness, and the feeling of having been used too often and seldom well.

She rinsed her body, turned off the water, and stepped, dripping, onto the fleecy mat. She turned toward the mirror and quickly squared her shoulders, arched her back, to pull her breasts high and firm. Of late when she looked at her body in the mirror, if the mirror was not steamed, she veiled her eyes and looked through lowered lashes, misting the image so that she saw only the trimness, the ripened daintiness. When vision was too clear she saw the parchmenting of the skin under her eyes, the sag of broken tissue of her breasts, the minute crenelations on the insides of her thighs. Deep tan could preserve the illusion of firmness better than a pasty whiteness. Deep tan hid the broken blue trace of veins on the backs of her calves, on the under portion of the round breasts. She toweled herself slowly, enjoying the erotic play of the towel's roughness on the delicacy of nerve ends.

Until quite recently the marriage had been endurable. It had never been good. Until quite recently there had been times when they had fun. Stay home and get a little high and laugh together. It was as though they felt young, with a lot of life ahead, a lot of chance to correct things. But they didn't seem to feel young any more. Something had passed by them. She remembered a time when she was a little girl, and her parents had taken her to New York. On a Sunday morning in the hotel room she had heard the clear gay brass of the bugles, the roll and thump of the drums, the music of one band blending into the music of the next.

She had waited with eight-year-old excitement and tension and impatience while her sleepy parents took an eternity getting up and getting dressed. They would not let her lean out the window to see the bands passing the end of the street. They did agree to skip breakfast and go watch the parade. They walked to the corner, Lenora dancing ahead. When they got to the corner the crowd was breaking up. The last band had passed. She caught a glimpse of it in the distance, all sheen and glimmer in the sun. She had wanted to catch up with it, but her father said you couldn't do that. They marched too fast. You couldn't ever catch up.

It was like that with Dil. The crowd was breaking up. Something went on down the avenue, shining and magical, and you couldn't catch up with it.

Ben Piersall had been the third boy to possess her, and the first one with whom it had been good. Between Ben and Dillon there had been several. Six or seven. For the first two years of marriage there had been none. And then it had started again. The first marital infidelity had been consummated on the bunk of a cabin cruiser anchored off a small island in Tampa Bay. Dil and the other woman had gone to cast into the tidal current at the south end of the island. She had stayed behind to nurse a hangover acquired at a dance the night before at the St. Petersburg Yacht Club. The man who owned the cruiser had come back to see if it was in danger of going aground in the tide change. And it had happened with greedy, ruthless quickness, leaving her with a feeling of shame that had not lasted, as she had expected, the rest of her life. It had lasted about three days.

There had been many other episodes. Some of them had been carefully planned. Some had been an improvisation of the moment. But not one episode had been calculated to achieve an advantage, to trade acquiescence for gain. Until Mooney.

She could not define her attitude toward Mooney. She knew she would never have entered into any relationship with him purely out of boredom or curiosity. It was not a question of social position. Mooney was probably much higher on the social scale than the big shy blond awkward young milkman of three autumns ago. Mooney had just not appealed to her physically. She had given herself coldly for the first time. She had half expected to be sickened by such an unemotional sacrifice. But it had left her feeling nothing. Nothing except an odd closeness to Mooney. It was a closeness not related to the physical but rather to an attitude, a personal reaction to life. In Mooney she recognized too many facets of herself. Slyness, opportunism, callousness. Plus a sensuality that demanded nothing more than the gratifications of the moment.

She knew that when she had been young she had not been like that. But then, probably neither had Mooney. No one began life with cynical appraisal. She saw that Mooney was, in many ways, ridiculous. But his absurdities were also her own. This sense of kinship had made the second episode far more stirring than the first. She knew that she was looking forward to seeing him today. She felt a thrill of excitement when she thought of it. Yet she was skeptical enough of herself to wonder if her anticipation was self-induced in order to rationalize the realization that this time, this first time, she was putting a price on her competent services—and there was a name for that.

As she walked naked into her bedroom, she heard the double chime of the front door. She slipped quickly into a blue robe and zipped it up the front. Jim Stauch stood outside the screen in the sunlight, blinking with lizard slowness.

"Hi there, Jim!" she said.

"Hello, Lennie." He came into the house, taking his hat off, wiping his florid brow with a white handkerchief. She walked with him into the living room. They were about the same height.

"I'm not expecting Dil for lunch, Jim."

He sat down and put his hat on the floor beside the chair. "I know that. Want to have a little chat with you, Lennie. I've been thinking about talking to you for a couple of days. I guess Dil won't like my coming here to have a little talk with you."

She sat down facing him. "What do you mean?"

"Dil's got himself in a little jam."

She made a face. "That's nothing new."

"You know about it?"

"Not about this jam. What is it this time?"

"Well, it's a little matter of a bad check."

Lenora had been sitting on the edge of the chair. She leaned back. She felt slightly ill. "That's a brand new kind of trouble. It's worse than usual. How much, Jim?"

"Four thousand."

"Wow!"

"It isn't exactly a bad check yet. It's dated two weeks ahead. I just don't think he's going to be able to make it good."

"I don't think so, either. What do you want to do about it?"

Jim waited a few moments and said, "I figure on collecting it, Lennie."

"How do you expect to do that? We haven't got that kind of money."

"You've got this house."

"I happen to know we can't borrow any more on it."

"That doesn't mean you don't have an equity. Myra's been giving me a bad time for a long time, Lennie. She figures I'm doing well enough lately so we shouldn't have to live back in the piny woods. She wants herself a beach place. We've been here a couple of times on parties, and this is the kind of place she wants. I want you to start thinking about it. If Dil can't make good on that check, I'll set a fair sale value on the house. I'll buy it and with the money you folks get you can pay off the mortgage, pay me off, and have enough left to put a down payment on a place of your own."

Lenora stared at him. "I don't think I understand. This is our home, Jim. We live here."

"Folks have lost homes before, and there's a lot of them that'll lose them in the future, Lennie. The ones that lose them are the ones that live too rich, live over their head. That's what you and Dil have been doing."

"You'll take it away from us?"

"I surely will."

"How did it happen? That check?"

"Little card game with the boys. He backed a hand real heavy. Backed it with bad checks. And it turned out second best."

Lenora got up abruptly. "God damn it!"

"I never liked to hear a woman cuss. I can't seem to get used to it."

"Jim, you aren't going to keep this a secret. You know that. Everybody in town is going to know you took our home away from us."

"I've thought about that, Lennie. I thought about it a long time. The way it looks to me, I don't think you two have so many friends in this town as you might think. Myra and me, we have a lot of friends. I think they'll say I gave you folks a break."

"Dandy break! You're so damn generous."

"It's a way out. What he did is a criminal offense. I could get him jailed and collect too, in the same way. All I want is the money."

She sat down again. "Why did you come and tell me this?"

"Your head is a little harder than his. You take a fellow like Dil. He gets in a bind and he pretends it didn't really happen to him. He keeps himself from thinking about it until the due date comes along. Then the roof falls in on him and he can't believe it was his fault. You plan ahead a little."

"But if you want the house anyway, what difference does it make, Jim?"

"I can use the house. I'd rather have the four thousand and no trouble."

"And no talk. That's why you came to me."

"I guess you've got it straight, Lennie."

She got up again and paced back and forth across the room, taking long strides, the fabric of the house coat whispering against tanned legs. She turned in quick appeal to

Stauch, hands outstretched. "What did I do to deserve this, Jim? Why does this happen to me?"

He didn't look at all friendly. He blinked his poached eyes slowly. "I can tell you, but you won't like it."

"I don't know what you mean."

He studied her, his expression mildly contemptuous. "You got yourself a man weak as water, Lennie. But he's husky and his disposition isn't bad. All you ever had to do was climb on his back and sink the spurs in his hide and keep them there. Good God, the way this town has grown it would damn near take a cretin to keep from making money out of it. But no, you weren't going to do that. He was supposed to take care of you. Put you in a pretty house and buy you pretty clothes. A man like that has to be driven. All you've ever done for him was sleep with him, and I don't figure he had any exclusive rights in that department. You've had yourself a lot of fun. People doing your cleaning for you. Sunning yourself like a country dog. Drinking fancy liquor and trotting out in the bushes with anybody that gives you the urge. At any time you could have sunk the spurs in him and rode him and made him make something out of himself. You're still a pretty little thing, and your looks have lasted longer than they should have. But the good times are over, Lennie. They're all over. You people passed the hump some time back and you're on the road heading down and you'll be surprised how steep and how fast the grade gets, and how far down that road goes. It goes way down, Lennie. You came along for the ride. You've had the ride."

"Damn you, Jim Stauch!"

"That's your style. Cuss me. I was just telling you."

She stood facing him. "All right. Suppose all that is true? Suppose I'm what you think I am. What can I do now?"

"Don't see as how there's much you can do."

"I'll tell you why you came here. You came from nothing. You come from bare-ass, hookworm cracker stock, Jim, and you've always been jealous of people like Dil and me. I'll remind you of a pass you made at me about twelve years ago. You weren't as fat then as you are now, but you still didn't appeal to me a damn bit. Now you have a chance to lean your weight on us and you couldn't pass up the chance to come out here and watch me squirm. That's why you came here."

His expression didn't change. "You might be right, Lennie. But you see, I didn't need anybody riding me. I didn't need spurs. I've made it myself." He picked his hat off the floor and stood up.

She moved closer to him. "Isn't there any way I can ... change your mind?"

He looked at her and half smiled. "Twelve years ago, wasn't it?"

"I think so, Jim."

He put his hand on her waist, slid it casually up to her breast, squeezed her breast with thick fingers. The pain made her wince, but she did not move away.

"Sorry, Lennie. I suppose that would be one way to work off four thousand dollars, but I'm so damn busy, I just rightly don't see how I could get out here to see you two thousand times."

She swung hard and he blocked the blow with his left arm, grinning openly. When she swung again, he caught her wrist and twisted it, spinning her around. He pushed her away. The screen door slammed behind him as she recovered her balance. She went to the screen. She called through the screen. The obscenities did not make him turn or slow his pace. As his car drove away she started to cry. She stumbled blindly through the house and fell across her bed, making sick, ugly, forlorn sounds. The crying lasted a long time. She felt stained and cheap and old.

When the tears were over she fixed her face. She went out to the kitchen and poured a big glass of milk. She leaned against the sink and drank it slowly, holding the glass in both hands, wiping the milk from her lips between sips with quick pink tongue. From time to time her breath would catch in her throat, the last meager ghosts of tears. She was no longer angry at Jim Stauch. She could understand his reaction. Her anger was directed at Dillon, and at Tomlin. Dillon was responsible for this. There would be time to punish him later. Maybe the house would have to go. But after they could get at the Tomlin money, it wouldn't matter. The first thing was to get the old man out of the way. During some telephone gossip right after breakfast she had learned that Hedges had spread his story quickly, had even embroidered it in the telling.

At a quarter to three she left the house and drove south down the key to the cabana at South Flamingo Beach. She parked the car in the hidden driveway and let herself into the cabana. She stood well back in the room and looked through the big window toward the deep blue of the Gulf. She arched and flexed her body, pressing the heels of her hands hard against the tops of her thighs. She smiled, and she felt cat-agile, rabbit-soft, mare-ready. Small spheres of heat seemed to rise up through her body and burst near her heart, like the bubbles that rise up through the pastel tubes of a juke box. When the spheres burst, it made her breath shallow and quick.

When she heard him come in she was breathing very quickly, and as she turned she knew that this time they would make the call she had planned quite a bit later. She saw his crooked grin and heard his rusty voice and saw his foolish arrogant strut as he walked toward her, and she moved quickly to meet him, her eyes half closed.

CHAPTER ELEVEN

Toby Piersall came home alone on his bike from school on Thursday, frowningly intent on his plans for the evening. Wednesday night had been a washout. During the afternoon he had crept close enough to see the big blonde woman sunning herself on the dock. After dark, after dinner, he had managed to get a lot closer to the Mather house. He had moved with great caution. He had found a window where he could see into the lighted kitchen.

He had learned nothing. At least, nothing that would enable him to prove or disprove his hunch about the man who called himself John Wheeler. He had learned that there were two other men staying there. One of them was huge. He had a battered face, but he looked sort of friendly and pleasant. The other one was younger. He certainly didn't look like a criminal. The way he looked shook Toby's confidence. If he was on a television play, he would have been the hero.

Toby, from his vantage point, couldn't hear what was said in the kitchen. At one point he saw the good-looking one stand behind the blonde woman and rub the back of her neck. The blonde woman didn't seem to like it. When the dark one came out into the kitchen, he looked angry. Toby had wanted to believe, when he saw the two strange men, that they were all crooks, planning something. But the two strange men looked so . . . ordinary. It was difficult to keep up the fiction. Toby was nearly willing to believe that they were what they seemed to be—people on vacation. He was half tempted to give it up and do his homework and spend the time that was left working on his boat model, the big one with all the parts.

He went into the kitchen as soon as he got home and made himself a thick sandwich and poured a glass of milk.

His mother said, "You seem strangely quiet, Tobe. Anything on your mind?"

"Num."

"Allowing for a quarter pound of sandwich, that must mean no." She cocked her head on one side and smiled at him. "Any big plans cooking?"

"No."

"Any trouble in school?"

"Gosh, Mom, I don't see why . . ."

"Okay, okay. Drop the rest of those crumbs out in the grass, please."

He went out into the yard. He moved over to the edge of their property. The big man was standing on the dock. He moved to where he could see the garage. The car was gone. He knew what he had to do, to get this problem off his mind. He had to see the dark man with his shirt off. The description had talked about the bullet wounds in the back of the man's left shoulder. That was the only way he could resolve it.

He rinsed the milk glass at the sink and went to his room. He studied the picture and description again, hid the clipping carefully away. He turned on his radio and stretched out on his bed and frowned at the ceiling. One way to solve it would be to give the police an anonymous tip. Harry Mullin is in the Mather house on Huntington Drive. Then hang up. He could call from the sundries store, from the booth there. The police would have to check. Or would they? He couldn't make his voice sound like a man's. Suppose they checked and it wasn't Mullin. Then he wouldn't look like a fool. Yet, if it was Mullin, how could he prove he had given them the tip? That was the important part. Brother, the school would really be jumping if he was the one who gave the tip and got the reward money.

It would be so darn easy if only the man would go out on the dock and take a sun bath. Then he could use his father's binoculars and find out with no trouble. If the scars were there, he could ride down to the police station on his bike and show them the clipping and tell them. Then they'd put a cordon around the Mather house and use a loudspeaker and tell Mullin to come out with his hands up. There might be some shooting. They might evacuate the houses on each side. Later, his picture would be in the paper. Toby Piersall, of Huntington Drive, son of Benjamin Piersall, prominent local attorney.

He wondered if he should tell his problem to his father. He would know what to do about it. But it wouldn't be the same. It wouldn't be the same at all.

Mullin was waiting when Ronnie and Sal got back just before dusk. The Ace heard them come in and he came out too. They sat in the living room.

Ronnie said, "Sally can check me on this. Joe Preston is a punk. He'll be no trouble. The nigger looks healthy and sturdy enough, but I don't imagine he'll make any trouble. The old man is frail. Preston's wife, Laurie, is probably the only one with guts. We both got inside the gate in the car and I got into the house. It's isolated enough. Nobody can see into the yard behind the wall unless they stop right in front."

"How about phone lines?"

"The line comes from the front, from a post out by the curb. It comes in over the wall. We can go in with a rock tied to the end of the rope. Heave it over the phone line and pull it down right away before we go into the house."

"Where's the box?" Ace asked.

"I didn't exactly get around to asking where it was. But a good guess would be the sort of study-library thing just to the left off the front entrance hallway. The old boy was in there reading. It will either be there or in his bedroom. I'll say it's probably the study. I don't want to put the hex on, Harry, but it looks easy."

"Then we can make it for tomorrow. Friday. Hit it about five or five-thirty," Mullin said. "Suit everybody?"

Ace shrugged. Ronnie nodded. The woman played with a bangle bracelet.

"We'll leave the car out at the curb. Sal will stay in the car and—"

"Harry," Ronnie said, "I think we can take the car inside. It will attract less attention. Blow the horn and the man will come and open the gate. He'll recognize it as the car that brought Joe Preston home today."

"Then they'll be able to give a description of you and Sally."

"They'd probably spot the car anyway and it would be the same thing. I think we can skip the masks, Harry. Move fast and shut them up so they can't get out, and be long gone."

"If you want to risk that, okay," Mullin said. "The Ace and I will wear the masks."

"Then how about the car?"

"We'll take it inside. While we're in the house Sal will turn it around and have it heading out. We'll empty clothes out of two suitcases and take them in empty. Round up the four of them in the study. From there we can play it by ear. We ought to have plenty of time."

"One man could almost handle it," Ronnie said meaningfully. "Two is plenty."

"Then why don't you go home, kid?" the Ace asked.

"Cut it!" Mullin said sharply. "Sal, go get some food started. We stay holed up here until we take off for the house tomorrow. Ace, we'll go over that map right now. Go get a bottle and glasses and ice, Ronnie."

"Yes *sir!*" Ronnie said. He followed the woman into the kitchen, patting the rear of her tight skirt as the door swung shut behind them.

"Stop it!" she whispered, turning away from him.

"You're a dandy bowler, sis."

"I like to bowl."

"Come here a minute, sis."

She backed away from him. He laughed at her and got the cube trays out and levered ice into a plastic bowl. He fixed her a stiff drink and gave it to her, and took the equipment back into the living room. Mullin and the Ace were huddled over the map. He looked at Ace's thick neck, at the small roll of fat, brick-burned by the beach sun, at the crinkled tonsure of ginger hair around the bald spot.

He looked at the Ace's neck and remembered the time in Brownsville. Rocco had fled to Mexico City and he was reasonably safe there, but he liked to return to stateside. It had taken a full month to take him. Ronnie had purchased the bench-rest twenty-two single-shot rifle in Houston. It had a special ten-power scope. He had broken it down and packed it in an outsize trombone case and taken the bus back to Brownsville. It had taken some time to get the right hotel room, a room on the eighth floor overlooking the walled court of a patio restaurant diagonally up the street. On the eighth night, two days later than the tipster in Mexico City had indicated, Rocco and party ate at the patio restaurant. They had come across the bridge in the blue and silver Cadillac. Ronnie sat on a straight chair in the dark room. Rocco had taken a convenient table. Three men and two dark lively Mexican beauties.

He remembered how it was in the dark room, rifle resting on the sill, watching the party through the powerful scope. It brought them vividly close, candles on the tables flickering inside the glass globes, the red lips and white teeth of the girls, Rocco leaning back when a great laugh split his dark tough face. Ronnie could have done it any time, but he waited. It would be awkward to shoot Rocco as he sat. The direction of the slug could be too easily traced. He watched the second round of coffee. Rocco began to look restless. He kept looking at his watch. As he made motions to get up, Ronnie cuddled the heavy rifle more closely. He allowed for the downward angle of the bullet. Rocco pushed his chair back and got to his feet. The cross-hairs were on his throat. As he started to turn, Ronnie touched the trigger. The spat of the rifle was lost in the traffic sounds. Rocco turned further, took a half step, caught himself and fell on the flagstones. Ronnie watched through the scope and saw a dark girl's mouth open wide in an unheard scream. People clustered around the fallen man. Ronnie dismantled the rifle and stowed it in the case. An hour later he went down on the street. He heard that a man had been shot through the head and killed. He slept well and checked out the next morning.

Looking at the Ace, he thought of the scene through the scope. He felt as if he were looking through a scope sight at the nape of the Ace's neck. Tonight would be as good a time as any. It would be some time before the house was investigated. Days.

Mullin felt as though he walked on thin places. When he walked across the room he had the curious feeling that the rug was unsupported, that it would sag under his weight and drop him into darkness. He seemed to feel a trembling under his feet. Everything around him had an odd fragility. The world did not seem to have the substance or purpose he remembered. It had been this way since he had escaped. He found himself touching things to test their hardness and reality. He felt at all times as if, directly behind him, there might come without warning a hideous, ear-cracking scream, a great yowl that would collapse everything around him, the way he had heard that a violin can shatter a wine glass.

This unexpected aspect of the world he had regained was something he tried hard to conceal. It made him unsure of himself and his own reactions. In concealment he moved slowly and his face showed nothing. The people around him shared the insubstantiality of material things. The Ace, Ronnie and the woman—they seemed for a little time out of each hour to be clever character actors, laughing mutely at him as they planned to trap him. He moved slowly on a stage. The world fell away off to one side of him, always out of sight. But there was no audience out there. There was blackness. The stage he moved on was garish. All colors were too vivid. And fragile—with nothing behind the walls until stage hands placed other rooms there. And the stage trembled constantly.

He felt an unreality in himself. As though he had ceased to be Harry Mullin, had become a creature quite different.

For a time he had been able to return to his own skin when he made love to the woman, becoming complete for a little while, finding substance and reality in a known act performed upon gasping acquiescence. But of late this too had become unreal to him, her buttery flesh an illusion, his own avidity a careless imitation.

And always, directly behind him, was the threat of the scream.

There was one way he could escape from this world that had become alarming. That was the reality of the money. He knew that when he had the money, when he could hold it, count it, plan how to spend it, he would once again be Harry Mullin, a man who could laugh, a man who was confident, a man who knew his place. Until then he was unfocused, a double image upon his own retina. It could not go wrong. It could not be permitted to go wrong.

At the evening meal he knew that the hours would be interminable until they would be able to leave the next afternoon. After the woman had cleaned up, she sat in the kitchen and listened to a small plastic radio, snapping her fingers softly when the music had a pronounced beat. The Ace and Ronnie played gin rummy morosely. Mullin paced the house. He went in the bedroom to get a fresh package of cigarettes. As he turned to leave he saw a whisper of motion at the dark screened window. He did not turn back. He walked casually out of the room. He hurried to the living room and said, "Somebody looking in my bedroom window. Go out the front and around, Ace. I'll take the back."

The men moved quickly and silently. Mullin's steps were soundless on the grass. After the house lights he could not see well. He saw the shadow move quickly away from the window. He heard Ace grunt, heard a shrill yelp cut off suddenly. There was a scuffling and the thick meaty sound of an open palm against flesh. He moved closer and saw that the Ace held a motionless figure.

"It's a kid," Ace said.

"Bring him in the house. Don't let him yell."

They took him in through the back door, into the bright kitchen. The boy's head lolled loosely and Ace had to support him on his feet. In the white fluorescence the smear of blood on the boy's chin was dark and theatrical. He was a lean brown big-headed boy of about eleven. He needed a haircut. He wore a T-shirt and khaki shorts and sneakers. He became steadier on his feet and his eyes cleared. He looked at them. His eyes were a vivid astonishing blue.

"You didn't have to hit him," the woman said indignantly. "He's only a little kid."

"Shut up!" Mullin said.

"The little son of a bitch tried to bite me," Ace said.

"It's the same kid was on the dock the other day," Mullin said. "What's this with looking in windows, kid?"

The boy backed a half step so that his thin shoulders were against the broom closet. "I was just walking around," he said too defiantly.

"Where do you live, kid?" Mullin asked.

"That's none of your business."

The Ace backhanded the boy across the mouth, knocking his head back against the broom closet door with a hollow thud. The boy's face twisted up and he began to cry.

"Where do you live?"

Before the boy could answer, the Ace slapped him again, harder.

"Where do you live?"

"N-next door."

"What's your name?"

"Toby Piersall."

"You're a wise kid, going around looking in windows. What's on your mind, kid?"

Mullin noticed that the boy was staring at his left wrist, at the scar there. The boy looked from the wrist into Mullin's eyes. He pressed himself back against the door and he turned pale. Mullin looked down at the scar.

"Learn something, kid?" he asked, his voice very soft.

"N-no sir. I . . . I . . ."

Mullin moved forward and caught the slim brown arm, twisted it in a cruel, punishing grip. As the boy started to scream, Ace clamped a big hand across his mouth. The two men stood close over the boy, staring down at him. Mullin nodded and Ace took his hand away. The boy was snuffling.

"You know who I am, don't you? Say the name, kid."

"M-Mullin."

"You're a smart kid. I bet you get good marks in school. So who else did you tell?"

"Nobody."

Mullin exerted pressure again. Ace muffled the shrill yelp. They kept at it for some time. Finally they stepped back. The boy slid down and sat on his heels, all curled up, head against his knees, shoulders shaking.

"Okay," Mullin said. "I'm satisfied. It was his own idea. His people don't know where he is. He didn't tell anybody. We're still all right."

"What are you going to do to him?" the woman asked.

"Glad to oblige," Ronnie said in a voice curiously high, tense and strained.

"Hell no!" Mullin said harshly. "We won't get cooperation if it starts off that way. Christ, who would get out on any kind of limb for us any place in the world if you start off killing a kid. Ace, go get one roll of that wide tape I had you buy. Pull those drapes across the windows in my room and put him in there. Tape him and gag him. Make sure he can breathe all right. Sal, after Ace tapes him, it's your problem. Check on him every once in a while. Listen, kid. You hear me? Lift your head."

The boy looked at him.

"We're leaving here tomorrow. We're leaving you in the house. They'll find you later. You got a big nose and it got you in trouble. But the trouble won't be any worse than it's been already if you don't try to get wise again."

After the Ace said the boy was all set, Mullin went into the bedroom and checked him. The boy was on his back on the floor in front of the closet door. He lay grasping his own elbows, forearms taped together from wrist to elbow. He could not reach the tape with his teeth and there was no way he could exert pressure against it. Tape encircled his ankles, and his legs just above the grubby knees. A wide piece of tape was pasted across his mouth. The eyes, full of tears, glinted in the light of the bed lamp. Mullin checked the tightness of the tape and grunted approval.

He went back out into the kitchen.

"I don't like it," Ace said.

"It isn't good. But there's no harm done," Mullin said.

"Sure," Ace said. "No harm. That's a big house next door. The kid doesn't come home all night. By tomorrow there'll be a big yell about kidnapping. Maybe there'll be road blocks."

"So there's a road block. The car isn't hot. My papers are all okay. We've got no kid with us."

"I don't like it," Ace said, his voice louder. "I didn't feel right about it at first. I don't like it. Let's get the hell out of here now."

Ronnie was leaning against the sink. He laughed. It was a bright boyish laugh. It broke the sudden tension between Mullin and the Ace. Both men looked at him in annoyance.

"Ace," Ronnie said, "you're getting old and soft and fat and slow. You should maybe get a new start selling brushes from door to door. Your brain is getting as soft as your gut. You're in bad shape."

Ace's face darkened. "Bad shape! Look, I . . ."

"Sure you're in bad shape. Look at the gut on you. Try this, Ace." Ronnie bent over and touched his knuckles to the waxed floor, not bending his knees, doing it easily, lithely, coming up smiling.

"I don't want to play games," Ace said in a sullen tone.

"You can't do it. So you won't try."

The Ace glared at Ronnie, and then he bent over, straining to reach the floor with his fingertips. He strained, getting a little closer each time. The other three watched him. Mullin, puzzled and frowning. Sally with blank face. Ronnie with a half smile. With a movement as quick and practiced as a dance step, Ronnie took the short paring knife from the drainboard and moved close to the Ace. As the Ace, alarmed by the movement, started to straighten up, Ronnie plunged the knife blade into the nape of the big man's neck.

There is no death more instantaneous when the thrust is perfect. The spinal cord is completely severed. All motors cease in that instant. The heart stops. The lungs stop. No dying messages can be given the great muscles of the body. It is as final as decapitation. The blade was at right angles to the spinal column, and the thrust was exact. Ace went from full-bodied life into the formlessness of one long dead. Perhaps the only awareness was a white flash behind the eyes, awareness gone forever before he struck the floor.

He raised himself not one fraction of an inch beyond the point where the blade struck him. He fell at once, sprawled, heavy, meaty face slapping the waxed floor. He did not move, twist. He was clay. Ronnie stood over him and did not breathe. Then he turned and tossed the knife into the sink. It clattered and came to rest.

"God damn it!" Mullin whispered. "God damn you!"

The girl was biting the back of her arm. Her eyes said nothing. She could have been stifling laughter.

"He was going to bitch it up," Ronnie said. He was breathing deeply, slowly.

"I needed him."

"You don't need him. You never needed him. Two can handle it. The old man will open the box for you."

"God damn you, Ronnie!"

"I was sent here to do it. That answer your questions?"

Mullin stared at him. "The Ace? Why?"

"One of the usual reasons. What difference does it make? We can handle it. The cuts will be fatter. He was about to crack up. It was nice and quiet, wasn't it?"

Mullin stared at the body. He sounded bemused. "Yes, it was quiet. It was that, all right." Ronnie knelt and worked the Ace's wallet out of his hip pocket. It contained a few dollars. He felt the thick dead waist, took the bloody-bladed knife and after pulling shirt and trousers out of the way, he cut the money belt loose. Mullin counted the money.

"Twenty-two hundred," Mullin said. "Cut it?"

"Give the girl the deuce, and it's ten bills apiece for us, if that's all right."

The woman was taking great pains not to watch them or look at the body. She took the two hundred, folded it twice and put it down the front of her blouse.

"Go in with the kid," Mullin ordered. "Take your radio along if you want to."

The woman left the room. They discussed where to put the body. Ronnie emptied the rest of the pockets. Then he linked his arms around the big ankles, and, bending low, dragged the body out to the utility room. He worked it behind the water heater and the water softener tank. He found an old grass rug in the corner. He unrolled it and tossed it over the body and tucked it around the exposed legs. Ronnie felt very tired. It was a warm comfortable tiredness. He couldn't stop yawning. He knew that his sleep would be deep and safe and perfect this night, like the dreamless sleep of childhood. It was always that way.

Toby was startled when the woman came in. She turned on another light. She had a small radio with her. She plugged it in and tuned it to quiet music. She stood over him, looking down at him. He looked up at her. She seemed very tall. Her face was in shadow.

She knelt beside him and put her fingertips on his forehead and smoothed his hair back. "Can you breathe okay, kid?"

He nodded. The act of casual kindness made tears come to his eyes again.

"You shouldn't have messed around those fellas, kid. They're too rough. I guess you know that. Your arm hurt?"

He nodded again.

"It'll be okay. Your ma and pa are going to be awful

upset about you, but it's going to come out all right. I won't let them hurt you."

She got a blanket from the closet. She folded it double on the floor and moved him over onto it. She took a pillow and got it under his head. She patted his cheek and then lay down on the bed, her head close to the radio. The music was quiet. By turning his head he could see her round arm and one upraised knee.

It hadn't been anything like he thought it would be. They hadn't acted the way he thought they would act. He had been scared when the big one had caught him. He had been hit and then it had been like being in a funny dream and waking up from the dream in the bright kitchen with them all looking at him.

It wasn't at all like television. Kids never got hit on television. Something always made it come out all right. The kids could be in danger, but nothing bad ever happened. Nothing like this. Somebody always came through the door with a gun.

He had felt grown-up and responsible, watching through that window. He had felt as though he were protecting something pretty important. But in the kitchen he hadn't been grown-up at all. He felt about six years old. Crying like a baby. If they were mad at you and hit you because they were mad, that was one thing. But these men hadn't been mad at all. They'd just done it. They didn't look as though they were even thinking about it.

It was Mullin all right. In the kitchen he had prayed that it wouldn't be. But it was. And Mullin had seen him find out and had understood.

He wondered what would happen to him. He wondered what they would do at home when they started to worry. He wondered what that funny noise had been, like somebody falling, and then a lot of whispering. Why were these men down here in Flamingo? Maybe they were going to rob the bank. He knew he'd been wrong about the other two. They were as bad as Mullin. They didn't look it until you saw them close, and then they looked even worse. He tried to get his fingers on the tape. He couldn't reach it.

And then, with sudden knowledge, with a heartbreaking awareness of self, too adult for his years, he knew that even if he could manage to touch the tape, he would not try to unwind it. He would not try anything. Like a small wary animal, he would merely try to endure.

CHAPTER TWELVE

At five-thirty on that Thursday, Ben Piersall received a phone call in his office.

"Ben? Dave Halpern. I think I've got a little on that item we talked about this noon."

"So soon? Good Lord!"

"It isn't conclusive, but it adds up to a little. Want me to come up?"

"I'll wait for you."

Lorraine Bibbs said good night and left. Ben waited in the outer office, the door open. Dave Halpern came down the hall and came in, smiling. Dave was a small gray man in his late forties. He had been a detective lieutenant on the Minneapolis force and had moved to Flamingo five years before because of his wife's poor health. He made an adequate living doing private investigation work and credit work. He was calm and experienced and reliable.

They went into the inner office. Without preamble, Halpern·began his report. "J. L. Mooney sells cars for Dil Parks. Dil hired him about Christmas time. He's a drifter. Yesterday or the day before he gave up his room in town and moved into a cabana out at South Flamingo Beach. Yesterday morning he visited Doctor Tomlin along with Lenora Parks. Today Lenora Parks left her home before three and drove to Mooney's cabana. I parked down the road. Mooney arrived about five minutes later. The two of them stayed in the cabana until about twenty of five. There was no time to rig a phone tap. The woman left first. Mooney left five minutes later. I let myself in. They'd been playing house. That was pretty obvious. There was a pad by the telephone. Here's the number that was written on the pad. 8-6861. Maybe it's nothing. I didn't check. I didn't hang around long. My status wasn't exactly legal.

I couldn't find out if she'd been there yesterday at the time that call was made."

"Let's check it right now."

Halpern leaned back and Ben dialed the number. A girl answered and said, "Flamingo Builder's Supply."

"Oh . . . Is Mr. Shannon in?"

"He's just leaving. I think I can catch him."

Ben held his hand over the mouthpiece. "Dick Shannon. It would be a good choice. Dick talks almost as much as Hedges. Hello? Hello, Dick? This is Ben Piersall. Say, I want to ask you something that may sound strange. Did you get a call from Doctor Tomlin today?"

"I sure as hell did."

"What time did you get it?"

"I'd say about four, maybe a little later. Ben, he's a sweet old guy, so they tell me, but they better come after him with a net."

"What did he want?"

"Wanted a hell of a lot of native stone. Said he was going to build himself a big house way out on Richmond. That's where his house is. I thought he was going to build another, and then he said he was going to get Tom Lowell to design it for him. Tom died back in forty-six. You know, damn it, he was talking about the house he's already got. When I got the point I sort of kidded him along. But I'm certainly not going to order that stone."

"Dick, this is a pretty delicate situation. I can't explain all of it. But you would be doing me a personal favor if you mention this to nobody."

"Why not? If the old guy is . . ."

"I'm morally certain that Doctor Tomlin did not make that call."

"Listen, I know his voice over the phone."

"Somebody was imitating him."

There was a long silence. "You sound as if you mean it, Ben. What is it? Legal stuff?"

"I may be able to tell you later, Dick."

"Okay. I'll forget it happened."

Ben Piersall hung up and nodded at Halpern. "Mooney

made the call. It's conclusive enough for me. I think that's all we need, Dave."

"If you want, I can put the fear of God in Mooney. It would be a pleasure."

"No thanks. This is enough. You'll mail me a bill."

Halpern got up. "Sure thing. Sorry it didn't last longer. And I'm sorry I'm ethical too. I could stretch this one out. I could go to Parks and sell him the idea of buying a little evidence against his wife. Say, I heard you used to go with her a long time ago."

"I nearly married her."

"Wow! You sure landed on your feet. Give my best to Joan and the kids."

Piersall sat alone in his office after Halpern had left. He wondered what he should do with the information. Dr. Tomlin was paying for the information and he had a right to know how it had checked out. But it was a serious responsibility to take. Tell Dr. Tomlin the story and the will would remain the way it had been signed at three o'clock that afternoon. From the icy point of view of impartial justice that was entirely correct. Lennie deserved no share of Tomlin's wealth. But Piersall understood her. She was not thoroughly evil. She was thoughtless and greedy and ruthless—in the same way a child is. She expected her world to be sequins and bangles.

He began to realize that he could not handle it impartially. He would see Lennie. Faced with exposure, she would stop. In a few days he would tell Dr. Tomlin they could find no evidence that Lennie had done it. Then the decision would rest with Dr. Tomlin as to whether to add a codicil reinstating the trust funds for his nearest relatives.

He phoned his home and got Sue on the line and asked to speak with Joan.

"Honey, I've got an errand. I'm going to be a little late. Okay?"

"It's chops. I can put them on when you get here, dear."

"And have a big fat dry martini in the freezer. This has been one of those days."

"Wilco, my lamb."

After-work traffic was thinning out as he drove out to the Parks home at Seascape Estates. The round sun was changing from yellow-white to orange as it slid toward the steel blue Gulf. The wind was from the east and the Gulf was flat calm. Dil Parks turned into the drive just ahead of him. They both got out of the cars at the same time. Dil came over, hand outstretched. "How the hell are you, Ben boy?"

As one of Lennie's previous boy friends, Piersall had always received a shade too much cordiality from Dil. They always beamed at each other, shook hands too heartily, both aware of mutual dislike, but intent on being more than civilized. Piersall's dislike was mixed with pity, because he, and most of the town, was aware that Dil Parks wore the most ornate set of horns in the area—large, curved, studded with brass and agleam with chrome.

They went into the house together and Lennie came in from the beach side to meet them in the living room. She wore a white sharkskin sunsuit, one cotton work glove, and she carried a red enameled pair of pruning shears. She looked industrious, plausible and glowing. Piersall found it hard to relate her to the cabana scene Halpern had indicated.

He had not counted on Dil being there. He had imagined his interview with Lennie alone. He sensed their curiosity as to why he had stopped in. They would know it wasn't social. His social patterns were quite different. Dil went out to the kitchen to make drinks.

"What is it, Ben?" Lennie asked in a low voice.

He made his decision at that moment. He told himself that he was doing it for her own good. He told himself that his dislike for Dil had no part in his decision. "I want to talk to both of you."

The drinks came. They sat out on the small patio. The rim of the red sun touched the edge of the Gulf. They sat in three chairs, three points of an orderly triangle.

They both looked at him expectantly. Piersall sipped his drink and looked at Lennie. "A lawyer has to do many awkward things, Lennie. This is as awkward as any of them. I'll make it blunt. On Wednesday morning you took a man named Mooney, who works for Dil, to Doctor Tomlin's home. Mooney met the doctor. On Wednesday afternoon sometime around three thirty, Mooney placed a call to Bud Hedges, the realtor. He placed it from a cabana he recently rented on South Flamingo Beach. You were with him when he placed the call. He imitated Doctor Tomlin and talked nonsense to Hedges. After the call Hedges started to spread the information that Tomlin was senile, had lost his memory. This afternoon around four Mooney made another call from the cabana. This one was to Dick Shannon. It was the same deal. Shannon thought it was Doctor Tomlin. You approached me early this week on the golf course and wanted to employ me to get Doctor Tomlin committed. I refused. Presumably other attorneys around town refused also. So you started this campaign to make Doctor Tomlin look ridiculous and incompetent."

He had watched her carefully as he spoke. He did not look at Dil. In the beginning she had looked dazed, and then defiant. Toward the end her head drooped and she looked smaller in the chair, smaller and helpless.

Dil came out of his chair with bulky speed to stand over her, fists clenched. "You and Mooney. A great idea! My God, you've really torn it now. I told you you couldn't work it. No. You have to be in a big hurry. Now you've spoiled the whole damn thing."

Her voice like a bright sharp lash drove him back. *"I've* torn it. *I've* ruined everything. Is Jim Stauch holding a bad check of mine? Do I owe Jim Stauch four thousand dollars?"

The anger left Dil's stance abruptly. "How . . . Look, it was just a . . ."

"Get the hell out from in front of me. I can't see Ben and we happen to be talking."

Dil walked back to his chair and sat down, his mouth working. Lennie said calmly, "Does Uncle Paul know about all this?"

"He suspected it. Today I wrote a new will for him. He was examined for competence by two doctors. Their reports are on file with the original of the will. He cut both of you out of the will completely until such time as your participation in this scheme could be disproved or verified, Lennie."

"God damn it, Lennie," Dil rumbled.

"Shut up. Are you going to tell him, Ben?"

"That's up to you. I think you've been a fool, Lennie. Conspiracy is a nasty word. The courts don't like it. I want you to give me your solemn word of honor that you will not continue with this scheme or anything remotely resembling it."

"You have my word."

"Her word of honor," Dil said.

"In that case, I won't tell Doctor Tomlin you didn't do it. I'll tell him we couldn't find any evidence that you did. Then it will be up to him to add a codicil to the new will if he so wishes."

Dil wiped his mouth with the back of his hand. "How much did she lose for us?"

"I can't tell you that," Piersall said. "And please understand, Lennie. I should have gone to Tomlin. I didn't go because I think you're foolish and greedy—rather than vicious."

"Isn't it nice to play God?" Lennie said in a quiet voice.

"Don't start that!" Dil said. "He's giving you a break. Maybe you can't get that through your head."

"Don't yammer at me. He's playing God and enjoying it."

Dil got up again, more pleading than angry. "Please stop it, Lennie. Don't get him sore. He can tell Uncle Paul and then we're cooked for good."

"He won't tell him. He couldn't feel virtuous if he did. That's Bennie's fatal flaw, Dil. He likes to feel virtuous. And stop ranting at me. You're the one who put us in the bag for four thousand dollars we don't have. Your poker pal, Jim Stauch, came here today and gave me the news. He's going to take this house. I guess you know that."

"Lennie, honey . . ."

"Don't Lennie me. Don't honey me. Just keep your mouth closed."

"I better be running along," Piersall said uncomfortably.

"Life among the savages makes you uncomfortable?" she asked sweetly. "Then maybe you better leave."

Piersall put his unfinished drink down and stood up. He said, "Dil, you better let Mooney go. You might tell him it's time to head north."

They were all standing, and as they moved through the big open glass doors into the house, Dil said, "I'll sure as hell let him go and fast. I never liked him anyway, and . . ." His face changed, seemed to grow heavier as a new facet of the situation occurred to him. He turned slowly toward Lenora. His voice was thick. He pointed his finger at her.

"Wait a minute. From his cabana. That's where you made those calls, the two of you. What the hell was in it for him? He's sharp. What was in it for him?"

Lennie looked at him and smiled. Piersall was shocked by her smile. She moved her body in a way that was just faintly suggestive and said with clear and unmistakable emphasis, "What do *you* think was in it for Mooney, darling?"

Dillon Parks made an astonishing sound. It was like the harsh bark of a small dog. He sprang at her, swinging his fist. It clubbed her on the side of the head. She flew sideways, loose-jointed as a boudoir doll. She fell against a basket chair that stood on slim wrought iron legs and went over with it, and rolled and came to rest face down, blonde hair spilled. She looked small and broken.

They both ran to her. Dillon dropped on his knees beside her and turned her over gently. Her eyelids fluttered and she opened dazed eyes and made a low moaning sound. Dillon sobbed and gathered her into his arms and stood up with her.

Ben said, "Is there anything I can . . ."

Dillon held his wife in his arms and looked at Ben. "There isn't anything you can do. This is between us. This is something we have to work out. I shouldn't have done that, but she shouldn't have done what she did, and we just have to work it out. Maybe there's a hell of a lot of other things we have to work out, too." His voice was unexpectedly steady and strong, his eyes agonized. "So all you can do for us, Ben, is just leave."

At the doorway, letting himself out, Piersall looked back. Dillon had turned to go toward the back of the house, and Lennie had slipped her brown arm around his heavy neck.

It was nearly dark when Ben Piersall turned in at his own driveway. The kids were in the front room watching television. Joan came out to the kitchen to meet him. She had changed to the type of clothing that he liked best on her, a frothy white blouse that set off the contour and texture of her good brown shoulders and round brown arms, a flaring candy-striped skirt. She kissed him and her eyes were fond. With pirouette and half bow she presented him with a chilled martini from the deep freeze.

"I fed the starving animals," she said. "We eat alone."

"I would even take you out. You look take-outable."

"And you look tired around the eyes, dear. Don't make major sacrifices. Your day was bad?"

"Lurid. Melodramatic. Maybe a day movie lawyers have. All the base emotions."

"I can hardly wait."

The night was warm and still. They ate on the side porch, stars showing through the overhead screen, candle flames moving slightly. He told her the events of the day. She was awed, amused, appalled.

Long after he had finished she said, "Ben, do you ever think that everybody else in the world is slightly mad? That we're the only sane ones? The only safe ones?"

"Sometimes. And then I feel superstitious about it. I want to knock on wood when I think about us."

"And when I look at you."

"The wench is bold."

"But of course!"

"Bold and pretty aromatic."

"This gunk is called 'Tigress.' And you're downwind. I planned it that way."

"Hmmm. I'm nowhere near as weary as I was, friend Joan."

"I planned on that, too."

They carried the dishes back into the kitchen. He went into the living room. Sue, on the floor, was making an intricate ceremony out of doing her nails, her history homework, and watching television.

"Where's Toby?" Ben asked.

Sue looked around blankly. "I thought he was here. Maybe he's in his room."

Ben turned the volume down and opened the evening paper. Joan came into the living room twenty minutes later. "Where'd Toby go?"

"He's in his room," Ben said.

Joan came back a few minutes later. She said, "Not there. Did he go out?"

"He didn't say anything about going out," Sue said.

Joan sat with her sewing kit, doing some mending. Ben found that he couldn't keep his mind on his reading. It wasn't like Toby to take off without a word. When he looked over at Joan she looked up at him, frowning a little. He knew that her thoughts were the same as his. He left the room. Toby's bicycle was still in the garage. He looked at the rack of fishing rods. They were all there. He went back into the living room and said, "Bike is there, and he isn't fishing."

"Maybe he went over to see Mike," Joan said. She put the sewing aside and stood up. "I'll give them a ring."

Ben listened to her voice on the phone. Toby wasn't with Mike. He heard her try another number, and then another. She came back into the living room frowning.

"I don't understand it," she said.

Ben left the house. He walked around the yard, walked down to the sea wall. The star reflections were steady on the still black water. A mockingbird down the street played infinite variations on a theme, his voice as silver as the star reflections. He stood in the night and called his son in a great voice, and listened to the stillness that answered him.

An hour later the last of his irritation and annoyance at the boy had vanished. It had been replaced by an odd fear. Both children were polite and obedient. It was Toby's bedtime. He wore a wristwatch and used it. He knew enough to telephone.

He tried to reassure Joan, and knew that she was trying to reassure him. But there was a flavor of fear in the house. It had infected Sue, making her eyes wider. Joan had called every person she could think of.

By midnight it had gotten very bad indeed. He could no longer retain objectivity for more than a few moments at a time. It was a warm night. Toby had decided to take a swim in the bay. But his trunks were not gone. They could not find his clothing. And he did not like to swim in the bay.

There were other possibilities. As a lawyer he had seen some of the men who had drifted into town. Degenerates. As callous and thoughtless as any animal. Night creatures, reeking of evil.

They tried to maintain the pretense of reassurance, but it was no good. Sue had been sent to bed, but she had come out again in her robe and she sat in a deep chair in the living room, her eyes wide and her mouth tense. When she had tried to make a suggestion, they had both listened and then snapped at her. Her ideas were too far-fetched.

He had run away. But he had seemed all right. Joan said he had acted strangely the last two days. Yet he would have left a note. And he would have taken his bike, and the money from his box in his bureau drawer, and certain small treasures.

At a quarter after midnight Piersall called the police. Lieutenant Dan Dickson, an acquaintance, was on duty.

"Dan, this is Ben Piersall. My . . . my boy, Toby, is missing."

"Missing? Did he go to the movies or anything?"

"No. He was right here after dinner. He walked out without saying a word to anybody. He hasn't come back.

He didn't take his bike. He didn't go fishing. He didn't go swimming. Joan and I just can't understand it, Dan."

"Ten years old, isn't he?"

"Eleven."

"I imagine you've phoned his friends."

"Every one we could think of."

"What time did he take off?"

"Some time after eight."

"Ben, has he wandered off like this before?"

"Never. It isn't like him. It isn't the sort of thing he'd do. That's why we're getting pretty . . . upset about it."

"Better give me a complete description and I'll relay it to the cars. Then dig up a recent picture and I'll stop out and pick it up and talk to you some more, Ben."

Ben gave the description. He hung up and turned away from the phone. He saw Joan's face and saw that she was close to the edge. He saw that she would break very soon. He did not know what he could do about it. He held her in his arms and felt the trembling of her body. He looked over her shoulder and saw his daughter turn her eyes away from them with innate tact.

"Steady, Joanie," he whispered to his wife.

Her voice was muffled. "I keep thinking. You said . . . about knocking on wood."

"Forget what I said."

"I can't help thinking about it. We said it, but we didn't knock on wood. Either of us. We could have and we didn't."

"He's all right. It's just something we don't understand. He's all right. Believe me."

"I can't believe you. I try to and I can't."

He could not tell her what he was thinking. It would deprive her of what little control she had left. He was thinking how he had played God that very day, how he had sat in judgment. Pride goeth before a fall. Things had been so good for so long. He had sat in judgment, in smugness and complacency, feeling superior to the troubles of others, convinced that his own star was soundly and properly placed in a sane known sky. This new black fear was

the price he was paying for pride and for a certainty beyond that which any man was entitled to feel.

Dan Dickson, big, young, mild, florid and bald, arrived
shortly before one, filling the entry hall, black leather belt
creaking, shield and buttons aglow in the lights, black
crosshatched pistol butt at his hip looking ominous and
official. He did not bring any reassurance or lessening of
tension. He underlined the knowledge that this was
Trouble.

He selected two of the pictures, sat and talked about
the boy in a low voice, made a cursory investigation of
Toby's room and left, telling them not to worry. It was
like telling them not to breathe.

It was some time after he had left that Sue fell asleep in
her chair. Ben and Joan lowered their voices so as not to
disturb her. Joan had turned out some of the lights. She
had cried, but now she was calm again, the calm of emotional exhaustion. She sat in the chair, her legs pulled up,
her face turned away from him. The lamplight modeled
the hollow of cheek and temple, the delicacy of brow and
jaw, the neatness of the way her head was mounted on
neck and shoulders. She was utterly still. The candy-striped
skirt was drawn tight across the roundness of her thigh.
One hand clasped her ankle loosely. He looked at the
picture she made there, and he felt a sudden harsh stir
of desire for her. It shamed him to feel that way at such
a time. It made him feel goatish, shallow and irresponsible.

The night was a great dark ship moving slowly by them,
so slowly that motion was almost imperceptible.

He awakened with a start and saw that it was after
three. His mouth was dry and sour. He got up and went
outside. Joan gave him a weak distracted smile as he left.
The coast was full of the stillness of the early morning
hours. All the houses except his were dark. Earlier in the
evening friends had phoned for news of Toby, but the calls
had ceased. Friends had stopped by and stayed for a few
moments and left. Ben would have encouraged them to stay
for Joan's sake, but she made it apparent that she too did
not wish their vigil shared.

He went back in and stood over her. "You ought to lie down," he said.

"I couldn't sleep."

"That doesn't matter. Lie down. It will rest you a little."

"If I should fall asleep . . ."

"I'll awaken you the minute I hear anything."

"Sue should be in bed too."

He woke Sue up. Her face was stunned with sleep, tongue thick. He told her they had learned nothing yet. He led his groggy daughter to her room. She leaned on his arm. It made him remember all the times they, the four of them, had returned from vacation late at night, the kids—much smaller then—asleep in the back seat of the car. They would open the closed house and he would carry the kids in, one at a time, small furry animals who smelled of sleep and made odd mutterings. In the morning they would not remember having arrived.

An hour later he looked in at Sue. She was sound asleep, a strand of hair across her eyes, fists under her chin. He looked in on Joan. She lay wide-eyed in the semi-darkness of the room. He walked over to her and she moved a bit to let him sit on the bed beside her. He took her hand. Her fingers closed tightly, convulsively, and then her hand relaxed in his.

"I keep thinking dreadful things," she whispered.

"Don't. Try to stop."

"He thinks he's so old and responsible. He's so little. He's only eleven. There's so much he doesn't know and wouldn't understand."

She cried. She turned and muffled the aching sounds in the pillow. She pulled her hand free. He put his hand on her shoulder and felt the tremors of her body. The only comfort he could give was to stay close to her. A long time later he walked out to the living room. The first gray light of day was over the world, a negative gray that made each leaf and branch stand out, as colorless as a faded photograph. The coming of day gave fear a different emphasis. The boy had been gone all night. He had left yesterday. The boy was gone.

CHAPTER THIRTEEN

The sun came up a little after seven in Flamingo on Friday, the fifteenth of April. A commercial fisherman, heading south down the channel through the morning mist, saw the angry round redness of it and saw how quickly it cut the mist and knew that this day would be hotter than any so far. This was May weather, not April weather. About seven hundred pounds of mullet, netted at night, made a pile that shone silver in the boat. The ancient marine engine chugged heavily and the slow bow waves spread toward the mangroves. Another half hour to the fish house. A man stood up to his waist in water on the grass flats, spin casting for trout. Birds dipped low over the water in the early light and the fisherman felt the sun heat on his cheek.

In room eight of the Spindrift Motel on North Flamingo Beach, a bride of ten days crept stealthily out of bed and shut herself in the small blue bathroom and looked at her tear-puffed face. The morning sun glared through the glazed window that faced east. She had cried each night of her brief marriage. She wondered if it was possible to cry each night for the rest of your life. She wondered if today she would find the courage to swim out and out and out—too far to return. It was the only escape she could think of.

Inland from Flamingo the sun awakened a young man in a station wagon parked in an orange grove. He faced the day with despair. It awakened an elderly man downtown, sleeping in a side yard under some pepper trees where he had fallen. It shone on a couple who ran hand in hand into the gentle surf and dived and came up laughing, their faces close.

The morning light awakened Mooney. He had awakened many times during the night when involuntary movement had caused pain. His face ached. It felt hot and swollen, particularly around his mouth. He ran his fingertips lightly over torn and bruised tissue. He ran the tip of his tongue across smashed lips, and used it to gingerly wiggle two loose teeth. It took a long time to get out of bed. His body was unexpectedly sore. He straightened up and walked slowly and heavily into the bathroom.

His face, in the mirror, was not as bad as he expected it to be. It was not as bad as it felt. The worst looking part was his left eye. There was an eggplant lump on the cheekbone, and the eye was swollen nearly shut. His lips were thick and puffy.

It had been a strange thing. He had spent the evening drinking beer. When he had returned to the cabana, he had seen someone sitting on the steps by the door, a thickset shadow, heavy in the darkness.

"Who is it?"

"Parks. I want to talk to you."

He had felt a quick rush of apprehension but kept his voice light. "Sure. Come on in, boss."

He had been in bad spots before. But he had always talked fast enough. That was the gimmick. Start talking. Throw up a smoke screen of fast conversation. He knew this had something to do with Lennie. Had she been damn fool enough to tell Dil Parks?

Parks followed him in, too closely. Mooney turned on the lights. Parks slammed the door. As Mooney turned, starting to say something, Parks hit him. He fell sprawling, scared and shocked. Parks didn't look normal. There was no expression on his face. Mooney didn't like the way his eyes looked. He was hit again as he started to get up. He was given no chance to talk. He tried to fight. The big arms and fists were like clubs. The room swirled and the floor hit him. Things got vague. The fists didn't hurt any more. They felt like big pillows. Parks backed him into a corner. He slumped against Parks, his head bouncing on the thick shoulder as Parks, grunting with each blow, drove those heavy fists into Mooney's middle.

Mooney's head bobbled loosely and he realized dimly

that this could kill him, and he wanted to tell Parks to be careful because you really could kill a man this way. Then he wondered if Parks was quite aware of it and intended to kill him. If so, somebody should explain to Parks that the woman wasn't worth it. But if nobody was given a chance to talk, how could you point that out?

The room swooped down into darkness, a great sliding dip like the first big drop on the roller coaster of long ago.

When he awakened blood glued his cheek to the floor. The door was open. Parks was gone. He managed to get to the bathroom and bathe his face. After that he was sick.

The woman wasn't worth it. Not worth a physical beating like this one. He stood in morning light and looked at himself in the mirror. The fat bastard had jumped him too fast, hit him just as he turned around. He'd never had a chance to fight back. Not a single chance.

Well, there's a lot of other towns and a lot of other agencies, and a lot of new sales to be made. Better deals than this crummy place. They sleep here all summer. They pass that same tired dollar back and forth. Time to pack and get out of here.

He told himself it didn't make any difference. It was just a beating. The body recovers. The swelling would go down. And things would be the same as they always had been. He told himself he was shrewd and sharp. He told himself he had a better life than anybody else he knew. Free as birds. Follow the sun.

But he found himself thinking unpleasant things and looking at himself too honestly. Take this job. He had hit three other agencies, bigger and better agencies, before Parks had taken him on. And take the women during the past few years. Some of them were pretty seedy. Face it. Casual pickups in cheap bars.

The jobs weren't as good lately and the women weren't as good. There wasn't as much money.

He looked at himself.

The next job would be no good. The next woman would

be no good. This had been the last good woman, the last one who would be fastidious, pretty, taut in her skin, fresh-smelling and desirable.

You are old, Mooney. It shows now. The clown face is aging. You've had the good years. Now the bad years will have you. And there isn't anyone. Not one true friend. Not one loyal woman. The bad years are coming, Mooney. They're here. You look like hell. You look like an old man.

The tears squeezed out of his eyes. He leaned his hands on the cold sink and looked at himself in the mirror and, from six inches away, he watched himself cry.

The orange-red light of the morning sun gleamed on the windows of the police department sedan as Dickson parked it in front of the Piersall home. His eyes felt sandy and his body felt tired as he got out of the car. He had been due to go off at four in the morning, but he had stayed on, puzzled by the disappearance of the Piersall boy. He liked and respected Ben Piersall. He wanted to be able to do a good job for Ben. He wanted to bring good news. But all he could do would be reassure them that everything was being done. He saw Ben Piersall appear in the doorway and, as he walked up the path, Dickson tried to shape his mouth into a smile of reassurance.

Very little of the morning light reached the utility room of the Mather house. It came through a high slit window. The rug covered the heap behind the water heater. Two flies were on the coarse fabric. They ran erratically, pausing, darting in one direction and then another. Their bodies were blue-green and iridescent. Whenever they came too close to each other they would whirl off into mock aerial combat, their wings whining. Then they would settle again to the fabric and continue their nervous search.

Lenora Parks awoke to the soft early sound of gentle surf. Dil was in her bed, close against her back, a heavy arm across her waist, his deep slow breathing stirring the hair by her ear. She felt a strange impersonal tenderness toward the sleeping man.

In the last few hours they had learned a good deal about each other. She thought she had understood him completely—all the weakness and self-excuse and childishness. For the first time she had dug down into the hard unexpected core of strength underneath all that vacillation. It had awed her and made him seem like a stranger to her.

She managed to disentangle herself without awakening him. The left side of her head, over her ear, was quite tender but she had no headache. When he had left her last night to go see Mooney she understood why he had to do it. She had waited for him. He was gone a long time. He came back with swollen hands and a look of emotional exhaustion. They had talked together for a long time. They had been completely honest with each other for the first time in their marriage. They had learned a lot about each other.

On this morning the Lennie who had sneaked off to be with Mooney seemed like an absurd stranger. They had confessed their inadequacies to each other, their fears, their trespasses. A lot of it had hurt. But it had been an odd hurt, like a cleansing.

Nothing would ever again be the same. Afterward, when they had made love, it had been like the first time. It was an affirmation. She had found the strength in him and knew that it was her fault that the strength had gone unused. She had weakened him by never meriting his trust, and by underlining his absurdities. She had made him a boasting clown merely by believing that that was all he was.

This was a day for starting new and fresh . . . and strong. This was the day on which she would start undoing the damage. No more betrayals. No more furtive affairs. It was a late start, but not too late. God, don't let it be too late for us. I have only him, and he has only me. No one else cares. Really cares. He has strength enough to forgive me. And so I have strength enough not to betray him again. Not to weaken him.

The sound of her shower awakened him. When she went back into the bedroom he was sitting on the edge of the bed, scratching the side of his leg slowly. He looked up at her with caution in his eyes.

"Good morning, darling," she said, and saw the quick effect of reassurance. She knew they would be awkward with each other for a time.

"Good morning," he said. He looked at his puffy knuckles, and flexed his hand. "I can't believe I did that."

"But you did."

"How much can I believe?"

"Everything that was said."

"About the house too?"

"The house too. We'll let it go. We'll let a lot of things go. We'll let the unimportant things go."

"And you mean it about working down there?"

"It should keep me out of mischief." She saw his face tighten and wished she hadn't said it. "I mean it would save money, Dil. I want to help as much as I can."

"I told you how it is. Maybe I can't hang on through the whole summer."

"You will."

"I hope it works out." He got up heavily and went into the bathroom. She sat and brushed her hair. She thought of how it would be. Loyal helpful wife. Faithful little wife. And, in the mirror, she saw her lip curl. It shocked her. Could this happen so quickly? After all the sterling resolutions? No, not this quickly. This was a temporary weakening. The strength would come back again.

But it would be so damned dull.

Was shallow excitement habit-forming? Maybe all this was phony drama, self-contrived in order to save her own face. Maybe it was over, and it would be better even to go along with Mooney.

She laid the brush down and looked at herself. She felt icy cold inside. She looked at her body. She thought, *maybe I have been too many times handled. I have known too much of lust. I have used my body as a pleasure-giving toy too many years. People don't change like this. People are what they have made themselves, and you can't turn back.*

But I want it to be different. I know that this is a dead end street.

He needs me.

But . . .

Laurie Preston was awakened by the subdued clatter of dishes down in the kitchen where Arnold was getting breakfast organized. She rolled over and looked at Joe's sallow face on the pillow. He would feel miserable when he awakened. He blew bubbles in the corner of his mouth with each exhalation and his breath was sour.

She remembered the couple who had brought him home, and she frowned at his sleeping face. They had reminded her of the people he had been with so often in California. They had about them the illusive stench of the illicit, the illegal. Joe seemed to be fascinated by that special odor. She wondered why. Did it make him feel big? Did it make him feel important? She knew that Joe could not explain it. Joe's mind had never gone beyond anecdote, had never advanced to the point where he could reason. He could argue wildly, but without reason. He wanted warmth, food, drink, a bed and a woman.

She looked at him and for the first time her doubt became a strong thing. She had had many minor doubts. Since she had been in this house, since she had been exposed to new worlds, she had often become irritated at the closed shallowness of his mind. All these new things that meant so much to her touched him not at all. There was no uneasiness or self-doubt in his scorn for the new things she was learning. He seemed bleakly amused—and became impatient when she tried to explain.

"So it's all in a book, baby. What's a book? It isn't real life going on in there. Just a lot of print. Come here, honey, and let's see how real living checks up with that book stuff."

And always he had been able to move her, to make the books seem unreal, to make the true reality that which she experienced in his arms.

Until last night. He had passed out when he was brought home. When she had gone to bed at eleven he had awakened. He had wanted her. She had been unable to dissuade him. He had used her body and for the first time she had lain passive, disgusted by him, disliking the touch of him, wishing for it to be over quickly. It had been a defilement, an animal using of something that had been precious and important.

She looked at the stranger who shared her bed, the stranger with crust of beard and bubbled mouth and acid breath, with his sleep-sweat of alcohol, begrimed nails and clotted eyes. Too often lately had she found him in the books. The people who wrote the books understood him and despised him. Steinbeck knew all about him. And Farrell. And also those long dead. He had been in all times, all places. The shallow animal, preening itself, using others, thinking only of itself and its pleasures, dead to everything significant in the world. Jaunty trousers and swagger and the glittering eye and the tattoo on the upper arm—ogler on every street corner—rapist in uniform—lyncher when the crowd was large enough—flexer of muscles—goat-boy, smug and bounding—but sidling back into the shadows, wary as a rat, when danger came.

And like all the others this goat-youth would change, grow thick and bald. With the quick flex of muscles gone, with the eyes dulled, with belly sagging the once jaunty trousers, there would be nothing left but a dull man with dull appetites and endless repetitive anecdotes of a youthtime that, in retrospect, seemed shining and gay and eternal.

I do not love you any more.

Once, when she had been about seven, Laurie had been invited to a birthday party. Fourteen little girls in a big house. She had not been dressed as well as the others and her present had not been as costly as the presents the others brought. She had not known the birthday girl too well, and she had not wanted to go. They made fun of her in the cruel sly innocent way of small girls. When she had a chance she had gone into the hall, taken her unwrapped present from the pile and had let herself out through the big door. On the way home she had scaled the coloring book into an arroyo.

It is time to take my present back and go home, Joe.

She looked at him for a long time. She was very fair about it. She remembered the several unexpected gestures of tenderness he had made. She remembered the best times when they had been together. She remembered the way he looked when he looked his very best. She tried to piece it all together again, and feel affection. She tried to want him physically. But it did not work.

It was completely over.

Goodbye, Joe.

She got out of bed. She washed and dressed and went downstairs to help Arnold.

Dr. Paul Tomlin was awake and heard Laurie's quick light step as she went downstairs. He wondered how he had lived so long in that house and not missed the sound of that light footfall. It had become so necessary to him. He felt a selfish guilt at taking up so much of her time. She was young. It must be stifling to her to spend so many hours each day with a very old man.

This existence would be perfect if Joe could be eliminated somehow. He was a jarring element. He did not fit. He spoiled the perfection of her. He was a smear of crayon across a good painting, a crack in a symphonic record. He soiled the girl. Perhaps eventually, had they not come here, he would have coarsened her beyond redemption. But that did not seem likely. There was a basic goodness and strength in the girl that made her invulnerable.

Ronald Crown came awake all at once and remained motionless, his eyes closed. He always awakened that way, reaching out with all his other senses to fix himself in time and space. Morning light glowed dark red through the blood in his eyelids. He heard the drone of a boat.

He remembered the Ace, the thrust, the fall.

It had been good with the Ace. Not one of the best, but good. The pleasure in this one was not due to the time it took, because it had taken very little time. The very quickness of it had made it good. All that sturdy muscle, and the big pumping heart and the big bellows of the lungs, and all the intricate interplay of secretion and cell-building and temperature-control. All the little electric impulses of memory and thought. All stilled. By two sudden inches of steel into the nape of the neck, severing the gray bundle of fibers in the spinal cord.

That had been good and the change in the other two had been good also, the way they looked at him. The uneasiness. The aroma of fascination. The way people speak in lower voices when they stand outside the cage of the tiger.

He opened his eyes and stepped quickly out of the bed, with no morning slowness, completely alert and coordinated. As he showered he grinned at the perfection of his own judgment of Mullin's reaction. Mullin would not try it alone. Mullin needed him. So Mullin could take no action against him. The odds had changed a great deal. Just Mullin and the woman were left.

Today was the day. He felt a fresh rising excitement. Between now and when he slept again, a great deal would happen. It would be a full day. Things could not be planned ahead. This one would have to be planned from moment to moment.

When Sally Leon awoke she heard someone humming in the kitchen and realized it was Ronnie. She heard Harry running water in the bathroom. There was a sharp odor in the room. She sat up and looked at the boy. His eyes were wide and miserable. He lay on the floor as she had left him. He had wet himself and the blanket under him.

"You couldn't help it, kid," she said softly. His expression did not change. "Don't be scared, kid. They're going to leave you here. People will find you quick."

But she saw a different image. They might not look in this house. They might not add the obvious two and two. It might be several days. And that would be too late for the kid. *Poor kid, he is probably awfully thirsty by now. Maybe Harry would let me get him something. Kids get thirsty and hungry.*

She put on a robe and went to the kitchen. Ronnie winked at her. "Good morning, glorious!"

It made her feel cold and funny to look into his eyes. "Good morning," she said weakly.

When she opened the refrigerator he came up behind her and put his arms around her, slipping one hand inside the robe to cup her breast.

"Cut it out!"

"I can't. I'm overcome. You're so lovely in the morning."

She twisted away from him and pulled the belt tighter. He laughed at her. She poured a glass of milk and took it into the bedroom. She knelt beside the kid.

"Kid, they wouldn't want me to take that off your mouth. But you ought to have something to drink. Here's milk. Promise you won't yell and get me in trouble and I'll give it to you. Promise?"

The wide eyes were on her and the boy nodded. She got the edge of the tape and stripped it off his mouth. It pulled the fine blonde hair from around his mouth and he winced with pain but did not cry out. She supported him with an arm around his back and held the glass to his lips. He drank the milk eagerly. When it was gone she lowered him again.

"What are they going to do to me?" he whispered.

"Nothing," she said. She put the tape back, pressed it down firmly and moved away from him as Mullin came out of the bathroom. He saw the glass before she could hide it behind her.

"What the hell have you been doing?"

"I . . . I gave him some milk."

He looked at the kid and then looked at her. "I guess it's okay. He didn't try to yell?"

"No."

"He's a smart kid. You are a smart kid, aren't you? Only this morning you don't smell so good. Sal, you want to try anything like that, you check with me first. You do that again and I'll rough you up a little. Check?"

"Okay, Harry."

"Why is Ronnie doing that damn singing? He feel good?"

"I guess so."

The sun climbed higher into the deep blue of the sky. Its color faded to yellow and then to a blinding white. The white sand beaches were glaring. Tourist flesh baked in the sun. A thousand bottles of lotion were uncapped. The young couple who had run hand in hand into the water at dawn were back out on the beach after breakfast, the private beach near their motel. She lay face down on a green blanket. He poured sun-hot lotion into the palm of his hand and greased the long smooth muscles of her young back, and the round calves and the backs of her knees and the backs of the firm thighs. His hand caressed her. They talked in low voices. The girl laughed. They got up and walked back to the room, laughing together, hips bumping together awkwardly as they walked over the loose sand, his arm around her in the first sequence of possession.

The bride felt better. The days were not so bad. In the daytime she could look at him on the beach and not feel badly at all. She wanted the sun to stay high. She wanted it to be daytime forever. Then life would be good. But, as it always had, the night would come, and she thought about it and felt chilled, even in the sun heat.

CHAPTER FOURTEEN

The bright day moved slowly along, like a carnival float going down a gay holiday street.

In the Mather house the three of them, Ronnie, Mullin and the woman, wore white canvas work gloves. They went from room to room rubbing their hands over everything that had been touched. Mullin kept them taut. He wanted no mistakes.

"And from now on you keep the gloves on until you're out of the house. Get it?"

"That's the fourth time you've said so," Ronnie said.

"I'll say it four hundred times. They'll identify the Ace. They don't have to be able to identify us. It'll give us more time. Sal, did you do the medicine cabinet?"

"Yes," she said wearily.

"Ronnie, go get the car gassed and have them check the tires and under the hood."

After Ronnie left, Mullin put Sal back to work in the kitchen. Keeping the gloves on, he turned on the radio. After five minutes of music the eleven o'clock news came on.

"A city-wide search continues for Toby Piersall, eleven-year-old son of Benjamin Piersall, prominent local attorney. The boy left his home on Huntington Drive some time last evening. It is feared that the boy has been kidnapped."

He listened to the description and the rest of the report. There was no mention of road blocks. He cursed his bad luck in having the boy recognize him. He wondered why Ronnie was taking so long. He wondered if he'd been picked up. The whole thing was getting fouled up. It had looked easy. Maybe he had planned this one too close. Maybe it would have been better to move right in on it as soon as they hit town. Or at least as soon as the Ace had arrived.

His stomach was knotted up and his hands shook. He knew this was the worst time. It would be better when they began to roll. Then there would be an outlet for tension. Waiting was bad. Waiting was the worst.

He heard Ronnie drive in. He went to the front windows, gun in his hand. Ronnie was alone. He put the gun away. The tension made him yawn.

When the phone rang again in the Piersall house, Ben grabbed it quickly. "Yes?"

"Ben, this is Lennie."

"Oh."

"Have you heard anything yet about Toby?"

"No. Nothing at all."

"I'm terribly sorry, Ben. I hope everything will be ... all right."

"Thanks, Lennie."

"About last night. That was pretty messy. I know it must have been horrid."

"It seems like longer ago than last night."

"I guess it would. I know how worried you are. I don't want to bother you, Ben. But I've got a crazy thing I want to do."

"What do you mean?"

"Call it self-punishment or something. I don't know. But I want to go see Uncle Paul and tell him the whole thing."

"That won't help any."

"I know it won't. It's like burning a last bridge. I know he won't forget it or forgive it. He isn't that type. But I want to burn our last bridge. Then we'll know we've only got our own feet to stand on. We'll know there's no pot of gold in our future. I don't think it has done us any good, planning on that money. So I want to put it out of reach for keeps."

"This doesn't sound like you."

"I know it. I want to know what you think."

"As a lawyer?"

"As a person. I don't know how to explain it. We're going to try to . . . start fresh. But it's going to be hard for both of us."

"If you think it would help, then go tell Doctor Tomlin. He suspects anyway. It might even give him a little respect for you".

"I want Dil to come with me."

"Does he want to?"

"I don't know. I haven't told him yet. But I think he'll understand. We're trying, but it's . . . so hard, Ben."

"It will be."

"Don't you think it's time I grew up, though?"

"If you can manage it. If you don't get bored."

"That's a low blow."

"I meant it to be. Would you mind if we cut this short? I want to keep the phone clear."

"Of course. Goodbye. And thanks."

"Good luck, Lennie."

Joan put her hand on Ben's shoulder. "What did she want?"

"She wants to confess. To Doctor Tomlin. For the good of her soul or something. She's trying hard to turn over a new leaf."

"Somehow I can't get very interested in whether she does or doesn't. Somehow I can't get the least bit interested in her problems. They seem rather small to me today."

"We ought to hear soon."

Joan shuddered. "They're searching the beaches. That makes me feel sick. Searching the beaches."

"Not only the beaches. Empty houses, fields, everywhere. Dan says even little kids sometimes get legitimate amnesia. They've broadcast his description all over the place, honey."

She spun violently away from him, shoulders hunched. She stumbled in the doorway as she left the room. He felt a weary helpless exasperation. What could you do? What could you say? Everything sounded wrong. There had to be an end to this. Some sort of ending. It couldn't go on this way.

Joe Preston got up at eleven thirty. He had slept beyond his hangover. He felt dulled and tired and very very hungry. He guessed that he would be doghoused for a time. But what the hell. That was a nice couple. And the girl had gone for him. She'd made that pretty clear. You had to have some friends. You couldn't stay locked up forever in this stone barn. Even in jail you could have friends.

As he reached the landing he saw Laurie coming up the stairs toward him. She walked through a slant of sunlight and she looked very good to him.

"Hey!" he said and she started in surprise.

"Oh, you're up."

"You look lush, angel." He caught her wrist and pulled her close to kiss her.

He expected reluctance. He expected her to look hurt and weepy. He did not expect the reaction he received. She yanked her hand away so violently that he nearly toppled down the stairs. She backed away from him, circling him on the landing. "Don't touch me!" she said in a quiet deadly voice. "Don't *ever* touch me!"

"Honey," he complained, "just what in the world is . . ."

"Be quiet. Don't whine at me. Just leave me alone."

He watched her go up the rest of the stairs, sturdy hips pumping under the cotton skirt, head high, not looking back. He scrubbed his head with his knuckles. He felt abused. What made her so mad? He'd just tied a package on. Not too bad a one, considering. What got into her all of a sudden?

He began to feel less abused and more angry. She was getting a lot of big ideas lately. Maybe she'd have to be knocked around a little. He'd never had to try that. But he'd thought about it. It was a weapon in reserve. It was a marital privilege.

He went on down into the kitchen. Arnold silently fixed him some breakfast. He sat at the table in the kitchen and ate hungrily as he read the sports page of the morning paper. In the back of his mind he wondered if he should go out and hunt up that pair again. Maybe it was a little too soon. Tomorrow would be Saturday. Maybe he and the girl could give that Ronnie the brush. Today would be a good day to stay in. Work Laurie back into a friendly mood. Maybe do a little work around the yard. That would make a good impression on Laurie and on the old man too.

At four o'clock in the afternoon, Dil Parks knew he had to call Lennie back. He had thought over her proposal until his head ached. She had some crazy idea about atonement. He knew how Uncle Paul would take it. It would be murderous. In a vague way he could see the sense of her idea. It made poor practical sense and good emotional sense.

She answered the phone on the third ring.

"I've thought it over. If you want to, it's okay with me. Maybe the old bastard might even like your doing it, but I doubt it."

"I have to do something positive, Dil. Like a seal on my good intentions. I want us to be absolutely without any resource but ourselves."

"You're going to get your wish," he said gloomily.

"Humor me. I'm a silly woman. Be strong and humor me."

"Sure. I'll pick you up about five and we'll go out there. But don't plan on me doing any of the talking."

"I'll do it all."

At five o'clock they were ready, Mullin, Crown and the woman. Contents of the suitcases had been bundled in sheets and piled in the trunk compartment. Empty suitcases were in the back seat. Mullin was satisfied that the house was clean of prints. The car was parked, heading out the drive.

Mullin looked at his watch. He looked at his hand. His hand and arm were steady. "All right. I'll drive it.

You in the back, Ronnie. Sal, you beside me. We'll take it through the gate. Got the rock and rope, Ronnie?"

"Right here."

"Once we're through the gate, you slide under the wheel, Sal, when I get out. Turn it around and head it out and leave the motor running. We'll come out fast. Slide over when you see us coming. Give one blast on the horn if we get company. Okay, get in the car. I'll lock up."

"Wait a minute," the woman said. "I want to go back in for just a minute."

"No."

"Please, Harry."

"Well, hurry it up then."

She went into the house. He stood by the open door. She went into the bathroom off their bedroom. She flushed the toilet and ran immediately to the boy. She stripped the adhesive harshly from his arms and wrists. She did not look at his face and she said in a low quick voice, "Wait ten minutes before you leave, kid."

She paused, as though to seek understanding or reassurance in the terrified eyes of the child. This was an act not carefully planned, but rather the result of slow resolve that had been growing within her since she understood that the child was to be left behind. Left in the empty house, perhaps not to be found.

Harry worried too much. Having the kid free would make no difference now. The kid looked too scared to tell a straight story, and even were he able to, they would be long gone before his folks could reason it out. It wouldn't hurt anything to free him now.

"Understand?" she said. "Ten minutes. You got to wait."

The boy nodded.

"Get on the stick, Sal," Harry called.

She trotted awkwardly back out to the front door. Her reflexes were not good and she could not move her soft body quickly. She went by Mullin. He yanked the door shut and tried the latch and followed her out. He got into the car beside her and put the garish ape mask on the seat between them.

As he swung the big car out of the drive onto Huntington he said, "You wearing a mask, Ronnie?"

"It's too warm today," Ronnie said in a lazy voice.

"Suit yourself."

"I plan to."

The dusty car moved through the late afternoon streets of Flamingo. People were coming back from the beaches, heavy women in shorts with red burned legs, brown young men with smooth arched muscular chests, old people carrying folded stools. Mullin drove carefully, precisely. They moved eastward out beyond the agencies and the used car lots, and turned into an area where the houses were farther apart, where some of them were the grotesque pastry structures of the boom of the twenties. The untended palms wore ruffs of dead fronds. They all looked ahead and saw the stone house on the left, the first story invisible behind the wall.

"There it is," Mullin said. "Make it cream and silk. We've got the time. Do it right."

CHAPTER FIFTEEN

Arnold Addams was walking slowly from the garage toward the rear of the big house when he heard the quick toot of a horn at the gate. He stopped and looked toward the gate. He saw the Buick and recognized it as belonging to the people who had come home with Mister Joe the day before. He wondered what they wanted with Mister Joe. Those people weren't too popular with Miss Laurie. But it wasn't his place to tell them to take off. Somebody else would have to do that.

As he approached the gate he saw that there were three people in the car. He didn't get a very good look at them. He swung the double gate open and the car came in so fast he had to jump back out of the way. Didn't seem as though those folks had much manners. He closed the gate and turned and saw the light-headed fellow trot over into the yard and throw a stone over the telephone wires. He couldn't figure out what in the world was going on. It looked like some kind of a game. The fellow held onto the other end of the line. When the stone came down he got that part of the line and gave a big yank and the phone lines came loose from the house and came down.

"Hey there!" Arnold said weakly, but with indignation. You couldn't have people going around messing up the phone. He turned as the other man came toward him. The other man had a face like an ape-monster. Arnold felt his heart try to stop as he backed away. He heard himself make a funny bleating sound. The ape-monster had a black gun in his hand. The gun swung up and Arnold tried to dodge back as it came down. The side of his head blew off like a rocket and he was down on his hands and knees, knees in the gravel, hands on the soft grass.

Mullin looked down dispassionately at the man on his

hands and knees. The eyeholes of the mask limited side vision. The rubber was hot and his face had begun to sweat. He pivoted for leverage and struck the colored man again with the side of the gun, struck the skull just behind the right ear. The man collapsed onto his face. Ronnie came over. They each took a wrist and dragged him away from the gate, over behind the shelter of the wall.

Mullin turned toward the car. The woman had turned it around. It moved toward the gate. He held up his hand to stop her there. She stopped the car. He nodded at Ronnie and they split, Ronnie taking the front door and Mullin taking the back of the house.

Mullin went in through the back door. There was a pantry where copper pots gleamed in the subdued light and the coolness. The kitchen was large and very quiet. He had to keep turning his head to compensate for the lack of side vision. He thought for a moment, then moved back to the door and bolted it. The odds were against their having to use the back door to leave. The bolt would delay anybody who made a break for the rear of the house.

His nervousness was completely gone. He felt very alive and very sure of himself. He felt strong and quick and completely impersonal.

He went through the kitchen again, stopped in a hall-way. The front of the house was brighter. He turned the muzzle of the gun toward a figure which came down the hallway toward him, silhouetted against the light. He saw almost at once that it was Ronnie. Ronnie moved close to him, mouth close to his ear.

"The girl is in the study with the old man. No sign of Preston."

"I'll hold them in the study. Go look for Preston."

He went to the study door. He heard Ronnie going quietly up the stairs. He looked in. The girl sat near the old man. The old man had his eyes shut. The girl had a big book open on her knees and she was reading to the old man in a quiet soothing voice.

Mullin watched them for a moment and then stepped into the room.

"All right!" he said loudly.

They both stared at him. The big book thudded to the floor.

"What do you want?" the old man asked. "Who are you?" There was a tremor in his voice. Mullin did not know whether it was age or fear.

"Just be quiet. Sit right where you are. Don't talk."

They continued to stare at him. The girl licked her lips. Her face was pale. Mullin stood and listened to other sounds in the house. Finally he heard a strange voice, querulous, complaining, and heard the silky sound of Ronnie's voice, heard them coming down the stairs. Mullin moved aside from the doorway. A young man stumbled into the room, catching his balance after a violent push from Ronnie. Ronnie followed him in and stood in the doorway.

"What the hell is this?" Preston demanded.

"Shut up and get over into that corner. That's right. Over there," Mullin said. "Face the corner. Down on your knees. Now put your hands on top of your head. That's right. Just stay there."

"What do you want?" the old man asked.

"I think you know, pops. You keep money around and sooner or later somebody is going to come and take it away from you. This just happens to be the time. So relax and enjoy it. Where's the box, pops?"

He watched them carefully. He saw the girl's inadvertent sidelong glance toward the wall on his right. "Keep an eye on them," he said to Ronnie. He went over to the paneled wall. There was no special effort at concealment. There was an exposed finger-groove on the sliding panel. He slid it open and looked at the box. It looked sturdy, with a heavy dial.

"Now you come open it, pops."

The old man sat straighter in his chair. His voice was stronger. "I don't believe I will."

"Now we've got a difference of opinion. That makes it interesting. I think you will."

The old man smiled. It was a confident smile. Mullin felt a reluctant admiration for him. There was nothing chicken about the old man. He said, "It so happens that I am the only one in this house who knows the combination. It is a very good safe. I am a retired doctor. You may know that."

"Stop quacking, old man."

"Just a moment. As a doctor I know the state of my own health. I know that if you attempt to use violence on me, my heart will very probably stop. And that will leave you with a very pretty problem, young man."

Sweat was running down his face under the mask, soaking his collar. It wasn't a nervous sweat. He felt calm. "We'll skip you for a minute while you make up your mind, old man. Come over here to me, girl. I want to talk to you."

The girl looked uncertain. She looked at the old man.

"Come on before I come and get you."

The girl got up slowly. She stepped over the book on the floor and walked over to him where he stood by the safe. Mullin looked at the old man's face, and saw the doubt and fear replace the look of smiling confidence.

"Closer!"

The girl moved a step closer to him. He jabbed suddenly with the stiffened fingers of his free hand, stabbing her in the solar plexus. The girl doubled up violently and moved back and fell to her knees, fighting for breath with a gagging sound. It was the only sound in the room, and it gradually quieted.

"Pops?"

The old man put his hands on the arm of the chair and pushed himself to his feet. His face was slack and old. "I can't fight that, young man."

"You want she should stand up so I can try again?"

"No. No, please. I'll . . ."

He was interrupted by Ronnie's sharp yell of warning. Mullin turned in time to see the book flying at his head, to see Preston on his feet lunging toward the fireplace, but not in time to duck the book. It hit him across the face, twisting the rubber mask, moving the eye holes so that he was blinded. He pawed at the mask with his free hand and got it straightened so that he could see. Preston, moving fast, came from behind the old man, came from an unexpected direction and Mullin saw the quick glint of brass as the fireplace tongs came down on his gun wrist. The gun tumbled across the rug and Preston pounced on it as Mullin stood immobilized by the pain in his wrist. Just as Preston started to straighten up, trying to reverse the gun in his hand, Ronnie, at last presented with a clear shot, fired. He was using the Magnum. The slug hit enough solid bone so that the foot-pounds of impact energy was transmitted to Preston's body. He went back as though hit by a full-arm swing of a heavy sledge. He hit the bookshelves solidly and rebounded onto his face. He tried to push himself up off the floor. Ronnie fired again. Preston's head suffered an obscene and sickening distortion. The gun-sound was a vast hammer-blow in the room.

"No," the girl said in a weak soft voice. "No, no, no."

"That God damn mask," Ronnie said.

"Shut up." Mullin tried to close the fingers of his right hand. His wrist grated. He no longer felt safe and sure of himself. He moved over and bent and picked up the gun. It was close to the dead hand.

He turned toward Ronnie. "Just a punk, you said. No, he wouldn't try a thing."

"No," the girl said again.

Mullin looked at the doctor. The old man wavered. His eyes were closed, his lips bluish. He staggered back. The girl caught his arm and helped him lower himself into the chair. The girl began to move toward her dead husband.

"Get back. Get away from him," Mullin ordered.

The car horn blew. Mullin stood very still. He looked at Ronnie. Ronnie's eyes were wide, his head cocked to one side.

"Go check it," Mullin said. Ronnie left the room. Mullin motioned the girl away from the old man. He went over to the chair. The old man was breathing in a funny way. His eyes were still closed. His lips looked like crumpled blue paper.

"Say the combination, old man. Say it now. Quick."

The voice was so frail he had to lean close to hear it. "Start at zero. Two turns right to eighteen, left to seventy-nine, three turns right to sixty." Then he mumbled something else.

"What did you say, old man?"

The voice was stronger. "I said may God forgive me for endangering others."

Ronnie came to the doorway. "A fat man and a blonde woman. They came through the gate. Their car's parked outside. They're looking at the black boy."

"Shill them in here. Fast."

He heard Ronnie's voice clearly. "You, out there! There's been some trouble. Would you step into the house, please?"

He moved back and Ronnie followed the couple in. They were in the room before they noticed the guns. The blonde woman put her hand to her throat. They both stared at the body. They turned as one and looked with disbelief at the fright mask on Mullin.

"What's going on?" the heavy man demanded.

"Shut up. Keep them in line. I've got the numbers."

Mullin waited until Ronnie had lined up the two women and the heavy man against the wall, their backs to the room. He went over to the safe. He peeled the mask up and wiped his dripping face on his sleeve. It was awkward using his left hand on the dial. Right to eighteen, left to seventy-nine, right to sixty. He released the dial and grasped the handle. The heavy door swung open easily. The look of the money took his breath away. There was so damn much of it. It made him want to laugh out loud. There was so damn much of it, the situation was ludicrous, absurd.

"I'll hold them. Yell to her to bring in the bags. All three of them."

The old man looked better in the chair. He was breathing easier. The girl was crying, softly. The blonde woman stood in a very rigid way. The heavy man shifted from foot to foot. The old man was staring at him steadily. Mullin suddenly realized the mask was pushed up off his face.

They came in with the bags, bumping them against the door frame in their haste.

"Pack it up," Mullin ordered. "Both of you. It'll go faster."

He heard Sal say, "Good God!"

He stood with his back to the safe, hearing the rustlings and thuds as they packed the money. He tried to think clearly about what they should do with these people. He had been able to think very clearly until Preston broke his wrist. His thinking had become fuzzy. There didn't seem to be any fight in any of them. The big rolls of wide tape bulged his side pocket. Strap them up one at a time. The one out in the yard, too. Haul him in where he wouldn't be seen. Lock the place up. It didn't make any difference that there were two more. The safe was open. The only one with any fight was dead. If the shots had alerted anybody, they'd know it by now. He tried to regain the calmness and certainty. He made himself breathe deeply and slowly. The wrist was going to be a bad problem. It was swelling badly.

"All set," Ronnie said.

"We'll all leave at once. Get the tape out my pocket."

"That wrist looks bad."

"It's broken, damn it. Get the tape. Take the blonde first."

He guarded the others. Ronnie made the blonde woman lie face down on the floor. She objected and he cuffed her twice and she submitted meekly. He taped her arms behind her, taped her legs at the ankles and above the knees, and put a wide strip across her mouth. The crying girl was next. She submitted with no protest. Ronnie took no chances with the heavy man. He slugged him brutally across the back of the head with the Magnum, taped him quickly and expertly as the man lay unconscious. The old man was next to last. They didn't move him from the chair. They taped his arms to the arms of the chair and put a strip across his mouth. It was a heavy chair. The old man would not be able to move it.

"Now all we got is the one in the yard," Mullin said.

"Want to check these? Fat boy looks powerful."

Mullin put the gun in his side jacket pocket and went over to the heavy man. He leaned over to see if the wrists were done properly. As he started to straighten up, something smashed against his head, dropping him across the unconscious man on the floor. He tried to scramble up but his bad wrist would not support his weight. He was struck again. He was not entirely unconscious as Ronnie taped him. The last band of wide tape was slapped across his lips and pressed down hard. He was on his side, arms behind him. He could see Ronnie's face.

Ronnie smiled down at him. He sat on his heels and smiled. Sal stood beyond Ronnie near the doorway, near the suitcases, her eyes wide, her hands clasped in front of her.

"You were going to be too much trouble with that wrist, old pal. This is a one-sided conversation. Too bad we can't have a little chat. You told me they'd never put you back in there. Now if you don't want to go back behind those bars, just shake your head no."

Mullin shook his head from side to side.

"Now nobody can ever say I haven't done a favor for an old pal. Nobody can ever say I'm not a thoughtful guy. You're never going back behind those big gates. Isn't that nice of me?"

Mullin watched in growing horror as Ronnie tore off a three inch length of tape. Ronnie leaned over and put the tape across his nostrils, pressed it firmly in place. He had taken a deep breath. With a convulsive effort of his lungs he blew enough of the tape loose so that he could exhale. As he emptied his lungs, Ronnie pressed the tape back in place. He could not breathe. He strained to take a breath. His throat and lungs convulsed. Ronnie's outline grew hazy. The room darkened. He made a last terrible effort, then the black blood burst behind his eyes, blotting out the world.

Toby heard the car drive out. He lay still. His hands were full of pins and needles. When the woman had taken the tape off, they had felt numb, as if they didn't belong to him. Now they hurt and the fingers didn't work right. He fumbled for the corner of the tape across his mouth. He peeled it free. It hurt to do it little by little, but it was better than yanking it off all at once. He couldn't make himself yank it off all at once. His mouth was sore.

He sat up, moving more quickly, and stripped the tape off his legs and ankles. It hurt too, but not as much. It took a long time to stand up. He was stiff and he felt high and tall on his legs. They felt wobbly, like a colt he had seen once, newborn. He had to lean against the wall for a while. If they came back, he knew he couldn't run. He listened to the silence of the house. One of them might be left. He couldn't be sure. It might be some kind of trick. He went to the windows. The outside air smelled good after the stench of the room. He unlatched the screen and pushed it out. He straddled the sill and tried to let himself down but he fell, jarring himself and biting his lip. He got up on the funny stilt legs and walked slowly across through the late sunshine toward his own home.

He felt strange. He didn't want to see anybody. He wanted to get clean and then be alone in his room with the door shut and be safe there, and lie there and hear the others moving around the house, and his father laughing and his mother singing, and even hear those dumb records Sue liked to play. He wanted to lie on his bed and look at his models. He wanted to grease his bike, and fish off the pier, and make everything just as it was before. But he sensed that things would not be just the same as they were before. There were dark things in the world. He had known about the dark things from far off, like in a movie or books. But not close by. When you knew about them from far off you could tell yourself that you could lick them. You could be quicker and braver and smarter, so that the dark things were conquered, as in the movies, in the comic books.

But the close look at them was much different. They made you into nothing. A bug on the sidewalk. They made you small and afraid and somehow dirty.

He walked into his home. He walked into the living room. His mother was on the couch. She jumped up and stared at him for a measureless moment, eyes and mouth wide. Then she was on him with wild cries, with tears that frightened him, rubbing her fingertips over the tape-torn lips, holding him tightly. Sue and his father came. They all tried to talk to him at once. He could not answer. His father silenced the others with a roar of impatience.

In the sudden silence he said in a quiet voice, "Where were you, son?"

"Next door. In the Mather house. They had me all fastened with tape so I couldn't move. Three men and a woman. The F.B.I. is after one of the men. I saw his picture in a magazine. I looked in their window to make sure. They got me. It was him all right. The woman gave me some milk. They're gone now, I think." To his own enormous disgust he began to cry helplessly. His father went to the phone.

CHAPTER SIXTEEN

The boy returned home at five-fifteen on Friday the fifteenth. Police entered the Mather house at five-twenty-five. The body was discovered almost immediately. The boy's identification seemed positive enough to merit advising the SAC of the nearest regional F.B.I. office. A description of Mullin and the woman was obtained from Hedges, as well as a sketchy description of the third member of the group obtained from the boy. Hedges fortunately had jotted down the number of the plates on the Buick. In compliance with the F.B.I. suggestion, and in line with normal operating procedure, the cooperation of the State Highway Patrol was enlisted and road blocks were established on Route 41, both north and south of Flamingo, as well as on two secondary roads leading to the interior of the state. These road blocks were in operating position by ten minutes of six, and were reinforced shortly thereafter.

All local radio facilities broadcast spot warnings to the population of Flamingo. A Coast Guard helicopter took off and began a patrol of the highways leading out of Flamingo. The news services picked up the item quickly enough to teletype it to all outlets nationally in time for six o'clock news broadcasts. All police officers in the Flamingo area were recalled to duty and all department vehicles put into patrol operation. The official assumption was that the group of three planned some unknown local operation, that the woman had released the boy sooner than Mullin had anticipated he would be released. Thus it might safely be assumed that the road blocks had been established in time and that the trio was inside the net. It was hoped that they would be apprehended before darkness made the task more difficult.

It was Lieutenant Dickson, the same officer who had

first been advised of the missing boy, who thought of the home of Dr. Tomlin as a possible target for the trio. He was with a Sergeant Moody in Car 6 with Moody behind the wheel. Dickson had been methodically considering the possible targets, the points of vulnerability in Flamingo. Banks, supermarkets, dog track.

"Turn right on Prospect, Lee. Just for the hell of it, I want to take a look at the Tomlin place."

"The doc? Hey, that's an idea. My old lady says he probably hasn't got any dough out there at all. She says people in this town talk too much."

"We'll take a look."

It was ten minutes after six when Car 6 turned down the block toward the Tomlin house.

Ronnie stood up and turned his back on Mullin's body. Sal stood by the suitcases. Her eyes were wide and they didn't seem to look at anything. She looked blind. Her lips were parted. Ronnie nudged her arm. "Wake up, kitten."

She started and focused her eyes on him. She shrank back from him. The reaction irritated him.

"Pick up a bag," he said. He took the other two. He turned in the doorway and looked back. The tape gleamed white in the dim room. It looked as though they were playing some strange game. He turned and followed the girl out. They went to the car. Suddenly he had a bad feeling about that car. It was a little too easy to spot. It had been used too much. He told the girl to wait. He went out through the gate and looked at the two-tone job at the curb. It was dark blue and light blue and had dealer plates on it. The key was not in the switch. He went back into the study and got the key out of the heavy man's side pocket. He had regained consciousness. His eyes were open. He breathed heavily through his nose.

Ronnie went back out. The girl was in the car. She had put the suitcases in the back. He opened the rear door and took two of them out.

"What are you doing?" she asked.

"You know the route?"

"Yes."

"I'll follow you in the other car. Take it slow and easy. I'll hang back a block or so."

"Why don't we both go in the Buick?" She asked the question too casually. She still seemed dazed, unfocused.

"I don't want it found here. When we get a chance to leave it, a good place, I'll pass you and stop. Let's stop yakking. This is taking too long." He looked at his watch. It was a little after six.

She drove out slowly. He swung the gates shut, ran to the other car with the two suitcases, heaved them into the back seat and got behind the wheel. He was headed in the right direction. When she was a block ahead, he pulled away from the curb. He reviewed the map in his mind. Five blocks ahead she would turn left. That would take her to the boulevard that led over to Route 41 where she would turn north toward Tampa.

He looked in the rear vision mirror and saw the police car coming up behind him. She had passed the intersection ahead. The siren started, shrill and terrifying, a shard of ice through his bowels. He braked and swung left at the corner, leaving the cruiser a choice. He looked back barely in time to see the flash of black and white as the police car sped after the Buick. He drove two fast blocks and then slowed down. If they were after the Buick, if they had it figured this close so quickly, then main highways were going to be no good at all.

He turned and headed slowly toward the center of town. He could hear the dying wail of the siren. He got the first inkling of an idea of how he would leave town, of how it might be possible to leave town. He adjusted the rear view mirror and drove on, carefully, cautiously.

Sally Leon tightened her hands convulsively on the wheel when she heard the harsh sound of the siren behind her. The siren seemed to awaken her from the daze that had dulled her mind as she had watched Mullin die. Never before had she seen pure nightmare. It was like the grotesque things that happened in dreams. Horror such as that could not be real, nor could Ronnie be a human being. He could not be like other people. He could not be sane. She had watched and she had been unable to cry out or try to stop him. She had been hypnotized by the look of pure evil.

For a long moment she let the police car gain on her. She saw the months and years ahead, the starch and the bars and the coarse denim, felt the bitter knuckles of the matrons, smelled the harsh antiseptics of the cell block, heard the way the inmates screamed at night.

She sobbed once and pushed the accelerator to the floor. The big car lunged forward. She was not a good driver. She took the corner too fast and the back end swung with a wrench and scream of rubber and she lost momentum. She held the wheel tightly and kept the pedal down to the floor. There was traffic on the boulevard. A pale pink panel delivery truck was heading east, a gray sedan two hundred feet behind it. She went through the stop sign onto the boulevard, and swung too wide around the pink truck, forcing an oncoming car off the highway to blast a frightened horn and bounce across a shallow ditch. She straightened out and began to pick up speed.

This, then, was the Dream. With the cameras picking up the speeding car, and the pursuit. This was the heroine, tears of fright filling her eyes, the road swimming toward her at thunderous speed. This could not be real. None of it could be real. The car was in a studio and it was being mechanically rocked while they dubbed in footage of a speeding road, dubbed in the tire sounds and the endless siren scream behind her. And these were glycerine tears. Soon somebody would yell *cut!* and the bored men on the high catwalks would douse the floods and light cigarettes and look down at the sound stage. She would go back to her dressing room, the table stacked with fan mail, and maybe she would lie down for a little while and rest.

There was another stop sign ahead. This time she touched the brake before she swung out onto the Tamiami Trail into traffic. She had good fortune in hitting a clear stretch between lines of traffic. She sped north on the two lane road. She risked a glance back. The cruiser was closer, not more than two hundred yards behind her. A line of traffic loomed up ahead. She swung into the left lane, directly toward oncoming traffic, holding it there, pedal to the floor. The oncoming cars darted off to her left, off the road, horns blaring. One did not move quickly enough. There was a small jar and clash of metal which did not slow her down.

Then the road was clear. Far ahead she saw the alternate wink of the red lights of a railroad crossing. Far off to her right in the very last of the sunlight she saw a purple train coming. The cars ahead of her had stopped. Cars coming the other way had stopped. She kept the pedal on the floor, knowing that she could reach the crossing first and angle back between the waiting cars, angle back into her own lane and be gone while the train blocked pursuit.

When she was yet two hundred feet from the crossing, the monstrous purple engine crossed the road. She put the brake to the floor and closed her eyes. The wheels locked. The skid sound joined the siren sound. The noise of impact was like a single sharp cough in a great brass throat. To the woman it was soundless. It was a great flash of pure white light, and she stood under the marquee at the premiere, having just gotten out of her limousine, and one of the reporters had come close to her to flash the bulb in her face as she smiled at all of them because they were her fans and it was never good public relations to be rude to your fans.

The train stopped a half mile beyond the crossing. The Buick was a tin toy that had been wadded in a big fist and hurled off into the palmetto scrub three hundred feet from the highway. Dickson was the first one to reach the car. He stooped and peered through an accordioned window. He saw what there was of her and he saw the money. He mopped his face and cursed. His knees were trembling. He looked back toward the highway. People had gotten out of their cars. They were darting back and forth oddly, stooping and pouncing like strange ungainly chickens. He could hear Moody shouting at them angrily. He started back toward them. On the way he picked up three twenty dollar bills and a ten. Moody could not control the people. They were picking money out of a field. Dickson drew his gun and fired three shots in the air. The people got out of the field, tucking the money away hurriedly. Dickson felt very tired. There was no way to get it back. One bill looked like another. There was nothing that could be done. Moody got the traffic moving while he went to the car radio. While they waited for the others, they picked up money. He turned and saw Moody shoving a thin sheaf of it down into his sock. He wondered if he should do anything about it.

"We interrupt this program to bring you a special bulletin. Harry Mullin has been found dead in the home of Doctor Paul Tomlin, retired local doctor. Mullin and his partner and a woman raided the Tomlin home over an hour ago. They knocked Doctor Tomlin's servant unconscious, giving him a severe skull fracture. They forced Doctor Tomlin to give them the combination of his safe. Joseph Preston, who with his wife Laura have been house guests of Doctor Tomlin, attempted to overpower the trio and was shot dead by Mullin's accomplice. During the robbery Mr. and Mrs. Dillon Parks, local residents and relatives of Doctor Tomlin arrived on the scene. The Parks couple, Laura Preston and Doctor Tomlin were tied up by the trio. After they were helpless, Mullin's partner overpowered Mullin and tied him up in the same manner. He placed tape over Mullin's face in such a way that Mullin died of suffocation. Doctor Tomlin suffered a heart attack during the robbery and is unable to give any estimate as to the extent of the loss, though it is known that he kept large amounts of cash at his home.

"Mullin's partner and the woman fled in two cars. The woman drove the car in which the trio arrived, and Mullin's accomplice drove off in a car belonging to Dillon Parks. Another bulletin has just come in. The woman was killed instantly a few minutes ago when her speeding car struck a passenger train of the Atlantic Coastline Railroad seven miles north of Flamingo, with a police vehicle in pursuit. And the Parks car has been found on a downtown street. Mullin's partner is at large in Flamingo. Make certain you do not leave your keys in your car. This man is armed and dangerous. Here is the description that has just come in. Blond, about thirty, slim, good-looking, wearing a dark blue sport shirt and pale gray trousers and a gray jacket."

Ronald Crown had checked into a bay front motel at dusk. He had smeared his prints on the steering wheel of the blue car, taken the two suitcases and walked three blocks and selected a motel at random and taken a room. He signed as George Peterson and explained that he had arrived in Flamingo by bus. He locked the door and closed the blinds and sat on the bed and lighted a cigarette. Every few moments his heart would give an alarming flutter. He took two loose shells from his side pocket and reloaded the two empty chambers of the Magnum. He felt betrayed. Yet he knew he was at fault.

He knew that he should have kept to his own specialty. Once the Ace had been eliminated, he should have left, walked out. But it had looked easy. Then it had started to go wrong. He should have known it was going to go wrong when they grabbed that kid. He should have known that Mullin was too stale and too nervous to handle any kind of deal, even this one. Then Preston had shown unexpected fight. And he had made a bad decision. It was too soft and it had taken too long to tape them up. They were witnesses to Preston's death. Once the safe was open, it would have taken seven shots. And he would have been out of there quickly, in the blue job. The timing went wrong. That much wholesale death would have created more heat than the Brinks deal, or that St. Valentine's day of long ago. But it would have been safer and better. And the money was worth it. That much money was worth anything. He felt a sharp pang of disappointment when he thought of the suitcase in the Buick. They'd get her quickly. They must have her by now.

He knew he would have to stop recalling how it had gone wrong, stop crying about it, and start thinking. This was only a temporary refuge. It came down to a very simple problem. Get out, with the money. His heart gave that unpleasant flutter again. The wall he was staring at seemed to lurch and dip and then rise slowly back into place. There was a new instability, insecurity, in all things. He thought of Harry, and he thought about death, and he thought about his own body stilled. He often thought of death in relation to himself. Many times he had grasped the warmth of his own arm or thigh, feeling the pump and thrust of life. Inflicting death had been a strong affirmation of his own living. A confirmation.

He shook his head sharply. Time to audit the vague plan, check totals and balances and risks. This was a refuge until full dark. Highways can be blocked. Trains and planes can be watched. But there is the wide darkness of the water, and a million paths across it.

At eight o'clock he left the room and walked away from the lights, down to the dark bay shore. Two hundred yards from the motel he found the boat. It was a wide-beamed sixteen foot boat tied to a dock with a stern line fastened to a piling. A large outboard motor was uptilted at the stern, with canvas motor cover and a lock that fastened it to the transom. The dock was behind a private home. He could see into the home, see a man reading a paper. There was a small shed on the end of the dock. It wasn't locked. He found a paddle and a five-gallon can of gasoline. He put them in the boat, careful to make no sound. He returned to the motel and got the two suitcases. He put them in the boat. He untied the lines. He used the paddle to push the boat away from the dock.

The moon was new and the stars were high and the water was black, with an oily look. He drifted on the tide past the lights of the houses and motels and the town. After he had passed under the causeway bridge, he used the bridge lights to take the cover off the motor. He used his lighter flame to read the unfamiliar starting instructions. There was gas in the tank. The husky motor caught on the third pull on the starter rope. Once he strayed from the channel and the gear housing bumped on an oyster bar, but the pin didn't shear. He found the pass between Sand Key and Flamingo Key and headed out into the Gulf. It was choppy in the pass, but more calm out in the Gulf than he had dared hope.

He went out until the city lights were dim on the horizon. He angled north. The night wind blew against his face, against his right cheek. Far up the coast he saw the lights of another city and he headed farther out. He hummed to himself, his voice lost in the motor roar. He grinned into the wind. He ran his fingers through his hair. Somewhere up the line he would land near one of those glowing towns. He would register at another motel. He would buy clothing. He would get a train or a plane. Or buy a car.

It hadn't been anywhere near as hard as he had expected.

CHAPTER SEVENTEEN

Ben Piersall played golf alone on Wednesday, the twentieth of April. The windless heat had continued. The fairways were baked dry. It was the first chance he had had to play in well over a week. His timing was off, his distance perception uncertain. He was glad of the chance to be able to play alone. The course was nearly empty. He teed up on the fifteenth and hit a towering drive over the fringe of trees toward the dogleg green.

Violence had come to Flamingo. Violence and greed that were strange in this place. News stories all over the country had been datelined Flamingo. *Time* magazine had done a full page on it under the heading of Crime: ". . . last Friday in a tall stone house in the West Coast Florida resort city of Flamingo, death came to lean, nervous, mask-faced Harry Mullin, murderer and thief. Forty minutes later his doughy blonde consort, Sally Leon, was smashed to her death against . . ."

Ben Piersall wondered if the town would ever look exactly the same to him again, if he would ever feel as he once had about it. Violence and death left a stain across the city. Flamingo, on that day, had become more a part of a rougher world. He knew that his own home would not be the same. The boy had changed. He had done more growing up than should be expected of an eleven-year-old. And they had all learned that they lived closer to the unseen edge of disaster than they had realized. Perhaps it would be good. It meant more appreciation of each day. But there was still an edge in their laughter, and the nights seemed darker than ever before.

His approach on the fifteenth was good and he canned a careful putt for the birdie.

It had looked for a time as though this thing which had struck with no warning had changed the lives of Dil and Lennie Parks. At least it had effected a reconciliation of sorts with Dr. Tomlin. Ben had talked with Lennie after the Joe Preston funeral. She had told him of her change in outlook. She had told him how she had changed, for good. But she took too long telling him, and she told him in too many ways, and even as she spoke he could see something in her eyes that had not changed and never would change.

Laurie would stay on with the doctor. Arnold Addams was recovering. The doctor would need more care than before.

As he walked down the fairway toward the eighteenth green he saw a group of his friends on the shady porch of the club house. He three-putted the green, much to his annoyance. He pulled his caddy cart into the locker room, mentally totaling his score.

Dave Halpern was sitting on a bench, a towel over his knees, a highball in his hand.

"How you doing, Ben?"

"I plumbered the round. Got in the trees on twelve and got a fat eight out of it."

"I settle for eights. You know, I keep thinking about that bastard, Crown. Even for a type like that, it's a bad way to go out."

"Crown? Did they get him?"

"Didn't you hear about it? They found the boat this afternoon. It was on the radio. Dan Dickson gave me the rest of the dope, the stuff they couldn't put on the air. He was about sixty miles off Fort Myers. They spotted it from the air and got the Guard boat out there. They figure he died sometime during the night. But he had been dying for days. Saturday, Sunday, Monday, Tuesday. Nothing aboard but him and a paddle and the money. Good thing it was so flat calm. He hadn't shipped a drop of water. Once they lifted that print off the back of the rear vision mirror of Dil's car and identified it, it was only a question of time until they got him anyway. But it's hard to say which would be worse. Dying of electricity furnished by the state, or dying of thirst and sunburn."

"What was he doing way out there?"

"You know they figured he was the one who took the Campbell boat. They think he headed north, pretty well out. Campbell said there was about two hours of gas in the motor, at cruising speed. So he was pretty well out when the motor quit. He'd taken a five-gallon can from Campbell's shed. Out there in the Gulf he filled the tank again. Filled it with straight oil. I guess when he found out his mistake, he tried to paddle toward shore. But the wind was out of the northeast. Dan says his hands were a mess. By dawn he would have been too far out to see any trace of land. The sun baked the moisture out of him. The body was probably twenty-five pounds lighter than he was when he took off in the boat. They think that toward the end he started drinking Gulf water. That makes it quicker. He must have been delirious at the end. He'd chewed on the corner of one of the suitcases, and he'd chewed his hands and his arms. All alone out there with hundreds of thousands of bucks, and with all that money he couldn't buy one damn glass of water. It's not a good way to die, Ben."

Halpern was gone by the time he'd finished dressing. The sun was nearly down as he drove home. Now it was all over, the last loose end snipped off. He drove slowly home to Huntington Drive and he looked at the Mather house as he drove in.

Joan met him at the door. The screen door hissed shut behind them as they walked arm in arm into the house.

MASTER NOVELISTS

CHESAPEAKE   CB 24163 $3.95
by James A. Michener

An enthralling historical saga. It gives the account of different generations and races of American families who struggled, invented, endured and triumphed on Maryland's Chesapeake Bay. It is the first work of fiction in ten years to be first on *The New York Times Best Seller List*.

THE BEST PLACE TO BE   PB 04024 $2.50
by Helen Van Slyke

Sheila Callaghan's husband suddenly died, her children are grown, independent and troubled, the men she meets expect an easy kind of woman. Is there a place of comfort? a place for strength against an aching void? A novel for every woman who has ever loved.

ONE FEARFUL YELLOW EYE   GB 14146 $1.95
by John D. MacDonald

Dr. Fortner Geis relinquishes $600,000 to someone that no one knows. Who knows his reasons? There is a history of threats which Travis McGee exposes. But why does the full explanation live behind the eerie yellow eye of a mutilated corpse?

8002